# An Old Tale Revisited, Sleepy Hollow, NY

Annette Desmarais

Published by:
Annette Desmarais, 2024

This is a work of fiction. Similarities to real people, places, or events are entirely coincidental.

**AN OLD TALE REVISITED**
**SLEEPY HOLLOW, NY**

First edition.  March 21, 2024.

Copyright © 2024 Annette Desmarais.

ISBN: 979-8224207268

Written by Annette Desmarais.

# Introduction

It cries out to the blood-red moon!
A mournful and eerie tune
Hoping for a change of fortune soon
But only hearing its own echo's croon

In the eerie moonlit Hollow where
shadows whisper secrets and fear festers
lies Sleepy Hollow – a hamlet cursed by a
chill not of winter but of the grave. Here,
beneath skies stained with the ghosts of
Hessian drums, echoes a tale as black as a
crow's wing. It is the tale of Ichabod
Crane, a pedagogue with eyes that
thirsted for knowledge and a heart that
beat for Katrina Van Tassel. Drawn by the

softness of Katrina's beauty and dowry, Ichabod unwittingly ventured into an elusive tapestry and became a thread in a gruesome loom.

As a curious and ambitious schoolteacher, Ichabod's thirst for knowledge and desire for Katrina made him a pawn and an obstacle in the Headless Horseman's quest for vengeance over his lost head. For Ichabod, this dilemma entrapped him in a terrifying conflict revolving around love, betrayal, and the supernatural.

Sleepy Hollow harbors a terror older than cobblestones, more fearsome than the wind howling through forgotten chimneys. Legends speak of the Headless Horseman, a spectral Hessian, his body a hollow suit, his gaze an infernal ember seeking its lost prize – his head. Every night, the hoof beats of his phantom steed pound the earth, a harbinger of ill fortune, a collector of screams.

Heed my words, for this is not mere campfire yarn. It is a suspense-filled chronicle meant to make someone's blood run cold. The line between man and monster clearly blurs in the mist, and laughter curdles into screams. Brace yourself for reliving the night Ichabod Crane clashed with the Headless Horseman in a conflict where love, betrayal, and death enmesh under a Blood Moon. Prepare to re-enter Sleepy Hollow, where truth hides in shadows, and the price of yearning is paid in hushed tones.

Graysen, a newly hired newspaper reporter for The Sleepy Hollow Gazette, lives his life deeply rooted in a fascination with the various legends of Sleepy Hollow. Drawn to the dark secrets and mysteries of the town, Graysen sets out to resurrect and delve into the petrifying saga of Ichabod Crane and the Headless Horseman.

As the owl cries out to the full Blood Moon, Graysen feels compelled to bring the chilling tale to light once again, weaving together historical accounts, eyewitness testimonies, and local lore to create a comprehensive and bone-chilling chronicle of Sleepy Hollow's most infamous legend.

So, let the old tale unfurl, once

again, in today's world, word by bone-chilling word, and remember, in the dark woods of Sleepy Hollow, there lurks a horror that has no face. Yes! The wandering soul of a dead Hessian warrior only bears a hooded cloak, a black steed, and a blade that gleams in the moonlight, a Blood Moonlight!

# Sleepy Hollow, NY

# (Chapter 1)

Fascinated by the legend of the Headless Horseman, Graysen read Washington Irving's classic tale, The Legend of Sleepy Hollow, many times.

When movie adaptations aired, he watched them, too! With a sense of suspense, trepidation, and outright horror always building, he would gasp, clutch, hide, and jump out of his skin through all the scary scenes. His hair curled when Ichabod Crane encounters the Headless Horseman on his way back from a party at the Van Tassel farm. Oh my God! He would suffer near heart failure when the Headless Horseman chases Ichabod through the dense and frightening woods.

Baffled, Graysen endured many sleepless nights trying to figure out if Ichabod escaped the Horseman or was carried off by the Headless Horseman to the spirit world.

For his 10th birthday, he celebrated

it by visiting the quaint little New York town of Sleepy Hollow. He toured the area with his parents and thoroughly enjoyed the historical sights.

Awe-struck, he stumbled when they came upon the 17th-century stone Old Dutch Church. WOW, a historical landmark! It is the oldest existing church in New York State and the second oldest in the country. Built in the late 17th century by Frederick Philipse, a wealthy merchant and landowner, it opened its doors to a congregation in 1697!

Emotionally overwhelmed by the significance of it all, he sighed and thought, "What a sight to set your eyes on!... The Old Dutch Church!! Oh, what a vision!!!" The stone building with a steep roof and a bell tower still had the little graveyard bordered by a wood fence.

Looking at it, Graysen could feel how the church's atmosphere takes on a chilling and mysterious aura at night when the moon casts shadows on the headstones and the surrounding grounds. The church, located on a hill close to a river and a bridge, supposedly is haunted by the Headless Horseman's spirit, who rides around the area looking for his severed head.

It is said that those who die an untimely death will forever walk the face of this earth seeking eternal rest. Well, the Headless Horseman is no different. During the American Revolutionary War, a cannonball shot his head off! Every night in the cemetery, his distressed spirit rises from his entombment and leaps onto his phantom black steed. As he gallops through Sleepy Hollow under the veil of darkness, he prowls and hunts to find his decapitated head.

The whispers of the town even warn that he will cut off someone else's head, too, which is why potential victims race to the bridge! They need to cross it before he reaches them!!!

How could this open threat to everyone's safety not leave everyone shaking with fear? Personally, Graysen felt this dangerous threat was nothing less than bone-chilling. It imperiled everyone in Sleepy Hollow!!! Yes, every mother, father, and all young people were at risk.

As his mind and heart felt emotionally burdened by these thoughts, he turned and noticed another critical sight.

Oh, the bridge!!! The bridge where Ichabod Crane met his fate.

Being a scared 10-year-old, Graysen reached for his parent's hand when he saw the famous symbol of the boundary between the real and the supernatural world.  His mind immediately started to relive poor Ichabod's unfortunate demise. To think, Ichabod reached this bridge, the bridge that spanned the Pocantico River, then a narrow wooden structure that creaked and groaned under the weight of the riders in the hopes of securing his safety. Yes, he so hoped to find safety on the other side, for the legend claimed that the Horseman could not cross the bridge. He prayed the bridge would not collapse or catch fire from the pumpkin's blaze.

Yet, with deadly accuracy the ghostly form hit Ichabod. The perfection and force of the strike threw him off his horse and into the river.

To envision the Horseman letting

out a triumphant laugh and turning his steed around only to vanish into the darkness left Graysen with a deep sense of pain for his friend, Ichabod.

The accounting of Ichabod's demise always left Graysen wondering if Ichabod drowned in the river, or as others said, he fled the town in fear or was spirited away by the Horseman. More importantly and a more contemporary concern, did the Headless Horseman roam the area at night?

For a 10-year-old celebrating his birthday, this prevailing fear of some headless night rider doing harm to him or his family gave him goosebumps. How will he sleep tonight...maybe between his parents?  Even still, though, he admitted, it was exciting to be here in Sleepy Hollow!

While touring, he and his family took special note of the famous Sleepy Hollow, NY bridge. While it is now regarded as a historical and literary landmark because of Washington Irving's legend, the legend's original wooden bridge no longer exists. Decay set in, and several other bridges over the years replaced the original one.

This current bridge is a concrete and steel structure built by William Rockefeller in 1912 and modified in the 1930s. It carries the U.S. Route 9 over the Pocantico River. It is near the Old Dutch Church and the Sleepy Hollow Cemetery. The bridge, though, is still known as the Headless Horseman Bridge and attracts many visitors who are fans of Irving's story and its various adaptations.

Still, some people hold onto the belief that the bridge is haunted by the phantom, especially around Halloween. So, Graysen, the now 25-year-old newspaper reporter, feels it is wiser to still pay attention to some old-timers' gossip.

# "The Beekman Curse"

# (Chapter 2)

At twenty-five, Graysen now got the chance to live in Sleepy Hollow. Yes! Mr. Shimmer, editor and owner of The Sleepy Hollow Gazette, offered him a job as a reporter. The local newspaper covers the news and events of the town and has been in business since the late 18th century. Mr. Shimmer, a flashy but kind and honest man, deeply cares about his readers and employees. His offer so utterly thrilled Graysen that he jumped at the chance to live and work in his favorite town.

After returning to his New York City apartment, he immediately started to meticulously plan and organize his move as well as terminate his lease. After dancing around his apartment most of the evening, he found sleeping difficult. So, as the sun began to rise in the early hours of a crisp autumn morning, Graysen started to hurriedly pack his belongings. Elated that his future no longer laid in this cramped apartment, he could not stop packing his possessions. Admittedly, his decision to leave the bustling metropolis was sudden and driven by an irresistible urge to escape the suffocating monotony of his urban life.

With having secured the writer's job at The Sleepy Hollow Gazette, no one could stop him now. No, no one could stop him from moving as the timeworn Ichabod Crane tale, whispered in hushed tones, captured his imagination since he was a small boy. No, he literally couldn't ignore the pull any longer. So, with bags hastily packed, he headed out of his New York City apartment's front door, jumped into his car, and drove to the small New York town of Sleepy Hollow in as short a time frame as anyone could orchestrate.

Sleepy Hollow is nestled within a dense forest and a meandering river.

It's always been known for its eerie history and utterly frightful, horrifying stories of the phantom rider who continues to roam the woods at night. If the existence of this night-rider doesn't leave you bone-rattling terrified, you will be interested in knowing the town's old cemetery supposedly is the resting place of those who have witnessed the Headless Horseman's wrath through the years. In this town, even the ancient trees reputedly whisper secrets no person dares to share.

Being intrigued by this haunting story as a child is one thing, but Graysen's friends and family now thought he was crazy to leave behind his promising career and vibrant city life.

Graysen ignored their severe criticisms. Instead, he summoned his determination to fulfill his yearning for adventure. With paid employment as a reporter, he could now afford to take the chance to explore the puzzling past that Sleepy Hollow held. The mythological landscape was now his to examine.

As Graysen drove through the winding roads leading to Sleepy Hollow, the landscape underwent a dramatic transformation since he first put the pedal to his car's metal. The views of towering New York City skyscrapers faded, and the thicket of ancient trees became the prevailing landscape.

Admittedly, the quaint small town's charming colonial architecture possesses a surreal and haunting beauty. While the scenery in this small town certainly was picturesque, Graysen couldn't help but feel a chill seep into his bones and a sense of foreboding as he drove past the town's welcome sign. He thought it was colder in the country than in the cement city. As he shuddered, he rolled up his car's windows and switched on the heater.

Slowly, he drove down Sleepy Hollow's main street, Beekman Avenue. Startled, he watched as the locals strangely stared and regarded him with a peculiar curiosity and caution. They stared at him as if his arrival foretold the future unearthing of something best left hidden, buried.

"Why, why are they staring at me?" he thought, "They are so weird!" Scratching his head and probing his recall, he wondered how the Beekman family influenced these townspeople so much.

As his mind started to recollect details about the Beekman family, he admitted that it was a fact that the Beekman family's darker and more mysterious legacy was hidden from the public eye. Wilhelmus Beekman, a merchant and politician, also practiced sorcery. He fervently sought the occult, magic and secrets, ancient rituals and arcane lore, hidden chambers, and secret societies. Wilhelmus also brought a book of spells and a talisman from Holland to build power and wealth. He also founded a secret order, the Beekman Circle, which consisted of his trusted friends and allies who shared his interest in the supernatural.

As Graysen inched his way down Beekman Avenue, he remembered reading about Beekman Circle's secret society of occultists and alchemists operated in Sleepy Hollow, New York, in the late 18th and early 19th centuries.

They were obsessed with the mysteries of life and death and sought to transcend the limitations of human nature. They believed that the area around Sleepy Hollow was a nexus of supernatural forces and that they could tap into these energies to harness them through various rituals and experiments.

The goal of Beekman Circle centered on the Magnum Opus, the Great Work of Alchemy.

It would grant them the perfection of body, mind, and soul. They yearned to become immortal, powerful, and wise, as well as unlock the universe's secrets. They also wanted to influence the course of history by supporting or opposing certain political and social movements, such as the American Revolution, the War of 1812, and the abolition of slavery.

Obsessed with the Magnum Opus, they worked to secure the promise to turn base metals into gold and grant eternal life. Generations experimented with various substances and processes, hoping to discover the elusive philosopher's stone, the key to the Magnum Opus.

Their heinous mansion was filled with hidden chambers where they performed their arcane rituals and tests. They collected rare and exotic ingredients, such as mercury, sulfur, saltpeter, and a mysterious substance known as dragon's blood. They used furnaces, special vessels used for heating substances, and alembics, which are used for distillation; crucibles, which are containers for melting materials at high temperatures; and retorts, which are used for heating substances in a closed system. They followed the ancient texts of Zosimos, Jabir, and Ripley, the Emerald Tablet, the Mutus Liber, and the Splendor Solis. They observed the changes of colors, from black to white, from yellow to red, and sometimes even the peacock's tail, a sign of nearing the goal.

But the Magnum Opus encompassed not only a physical process but also a spiritual one. It required the purification and transformation of the soul and the body. The Beekmans, however, were blinded by their greed and pride. They ignored alchemy's moral and ethical aspects and focused only on the material and temporal benefits. They performed gruesome rituals, sacrificed animals, and even humans, to obtain their blood and vital essence. They made deals with the devil and invoked dark forces to aid them in their quest.

Little did they know they were about to be engulfed by a dark and ominous force beyond their comprehension. Yes, they were playing with fire and would soon be consumed by it. During a thunderstorm one night, they attempted the final stage of the Magnum Opus, the projection of the philosopher's stone onto a base metal. After years of trial and error, they obtained a small amount of the red powder, which they believed to be the stone. They placed it in a crucible with some lead and heated it over a fire. They expected to see a flash of light and then a mass of pure gold.

But instead, they saw a blast of flames and then a cloud of billowing smoke. The crucible exploded, and the powder ignited. The fire spread quickly, engulfing the grand estate and its inhabitants. The Beekmans screamed in agony as the engulfing inferno caused their flesh to melt and their bones to crack. They realized too late that they had been tragically deceived. Their powder was not the philosopher's stone but a deadly explosive. They failed in their quest to achieve the Magnum Opus but the opposite: the Magnum Chaos, the Great Destruction.

The Hades hellfire raged for hours! Nothing remained of the Beekman mansion but ashes and rubble. Shocked and terrified, the Sleepy Hollow villagers witnessed the ball of fire from a safe distance. They wondered what caused such a catastrophe and what secrets the Beekmans had hidden. Some said that they had seen strange shapes and shadows in the flames. They also heard unearthly noises and voices. Some said they had seen the devil himself, laughing and dancing among the ruins.

The legend of Beekman's Magnum Opus soon spread throughout the region, becoming a source of fear and fascination for many. Some brave or foolish adventurers tried to explore the disaster site, hoping to find some clues or treasures. But they always returned empty-handed or not at all. Haunted by Beekman ghosts, their spectral forms now seek the philosopher's stone. Anyone who ventures there would meet a horrible fate. The place is cursed!

And so, even today, the Beekman's Magnum Opus remains a mystery; the Beekman's story holds a warning for those who dared to tamper with the secrets of nature and the laws of God.

Seeking to unlock the universe's secrets for generations, the Beekman Circle continued passing down their knowledge, expertise, and the secrets they discovered to their heirs.

Enemies like the Hessian army tried to find them to expose and kill them. Also, they had numerous bad encounters with the supernatural, including vampires, werewolves, witches, demons, and ghosts.

No documented records exist since the Beekman Circle's secret history was only whispered among its members. People suspect the secrets and magic resided deep within the former Beekman homestead.

Folklore claims the wealthy landowners made a pact with the devil to keep the Native Americans and the British from stealing their land. As part of the pact, they presented to the devil each year on Halloween one of their own's beheaded head.

While they successfully kept its history a secret for generations, they still lived in fear of people detouring through the woods where they might witness the Circle's ritual of dragging a hooded figure to a stone altar and chopping off his head with an axe.

With this sacrificial practice exposed, the townspeople, outraged, would rise, storm their residences, and burn them to the ground. With a sense of deep vengeance, they would hang Beekman Circle members from the trees and throw their heads into the river. After discussing these consequences, the Circle solemnly vowed to never speak of their history again!

# This Befell Me!

## (Chapter 3)

When Graysen arrived in town at dusk, the weather was cold, damp, and foggy. He decided to continue driving slowly and explore the town's main street for a bit more time.

Feeling hungry, he wondered what old-world restaurants offered an early dinner? Wouldn't it be fun to enjoy a wonderfully colonial-styled dinner on his first night in his new hometown? After all, Sleepy Hollow was a charming and historic place full of unique and memorable shops, restaurants, and even museums. It most definitely must offer interesting restaurants for dining.

Since the fog made it difficult to see, he parked his car and set out to walk along the sidewalk. The town clock towered over everything, with a scarecrow dressed as Jack of Jack-o-lantern. It looked like a creepy decoration for Halloween. Still, Graysen wondered if it held any significance to the Headless Horseman's roamings. As he continued on his footpath, the reporter within him continued studying the old buildings and the orange street signs with a sense of intrigue. Did any of these establishments have anything to do with the town's belief that the Headless Horseman prowls their streets at night looking for his lost head? Remember, too, that Halloween is a big night for the Headless Horseman. As he passed a bookstore, he noticed a sign that said, "Welcome To Sleepy Hollow Horror Stories." The store's name caught his eye as a reporter and avid reader. He immediately stopped and decided to duck in to check it out.

Graysen found the shop small and dusty, with shelves full of books and magazines. The counter held the old-styled cash register, and a few chairs surrounded the counter. Behind the counter, an old man with a long beard and glasses sat. He looked up from his book and smiled.

"Hello there!" he bellowed. "Welcome to Sleepy Hollow Horror Stories! Are you looking for something in particular?" and followed his question up with a ghoulish laugh.

Graysen shrugged, "No, I am new in town. Today is my first day, to be more specific. I am just trying to get to know the shops I will rely on for stuff. I am also the new reporter at The Sleepy Hollow Gazette. The book you are holding, yes, the one about the Headless Horseman, is one of my favorites. I even had my parents bring me to Sleepy Hollow for my 10th birthday because of your town's legend."

The shopkeeper nodded in agreement and then reached under his counter. Out, he pulled a book with a skull on the cover. "This, this is where it all began," he said. "The story of how Ichabod Crane became the victim of the Headless Horseman."

As he handed Graysen the book, he opened it to a page marked with a bookmark. "Here's how it goes," he said. "It's quite gruesome! Just thought that I'd warn you."

Graysen took the book and looked at the page. It read:

"Ichabod Crane was an educated man who came to Sleepy Hollow from Connecticut seeking fame and fortune. He heard of the town's reputation as a place where strange things happened but did not believe in such nonsense.

He rented a room at the Van Tassel house, where he met the beautiful Peggy. She, the daughter of the wealthy farmer Baltus Van Tassel, who owned the home, was also the sister of Katrina Van Tassel, the beautiful and coquettish heiress who was courted by many, including Brom Bones Van Brunt. Peggy, described as a "plump and blooming lass of fresh eighteen," loved to dance and flirt with the young men at the harvest feast.

Quite taken with Ichabod upon meeting him, Peggy immediately fell in love with him at first sight.

Brom Bones, Peggy's cousin, made it his business to warn Ichabod, the skeptic, about the dangers of Sleepy Hollow at their first meeting.

One night, Ichabod went for a walk in the woods near his house. He saw a man riding on horseback without a head. He thought it was an illusion caused by his imagination or some prankster playing tricks on him.

The next day, he went to visit Peggy at her house. He found her unconscious, lying on her bed. There was blood everywhere but no sign of cuts, struggle, or even a robbery.

Shocked and terrified by what he saw, Ichabod ran out of the house and into the woods again. He hoped to find some clues or witnesses that could explain what happened.  Instead of finding answers, he found more horror. He saw yet again a man riding on horseback without a head.  This time, he realized it was not an illusion or a prank.  It was real, and it was coming for him."

Graysen felt goosebumps as he read the story. It was so vivid and terrifying that he almost dropped the book. "WOW!!!" he said to himself.

The old man nodded in agreement and said, "That's right, that's how it all started."

He closed his book and put it back under the counter. "But don't worry," he said with a smile. "It's just fiction." "Or is it?" he said with an unnerving wink. Graysen looked at him with confusion.

Feeling dizzy, Graysen turned away from the old man just before he asked him, "What do you mean?" The old man leaned closer behind Graysen and whispered in his ear. "I mean that maybe, well, maybe you're next!"

Graysen felt his breath on his neck and shivered. Still looking away, Graysen nervously asked, "What are you talking about?"

The old shopkeeper chuckled softly. "I'm talking about Sleepy Hollow's curse," he said.

Perplexed, Graysen turned back

around to face him, whereupon the shopkeeper pointed at his own headless neck. "You see this?" he asked Graysen.

In shock, Graysen slowly nodded as he struggled to remain standing. "Yes," Graysen fearfully whispered. "Well," the shopkeeper said slowly, "This befell me!"

Totally terrorized, Graysen somehow managed to move his mouth into a smile. He so wanted to believe that the old man's changed appearance was a very old Sleepy Hollow shopkeeper's magician's trick that he pulled when Graysen turned away.

Oh, the name of the book with the skull on it? The Curse.

Upon exiting the shop, the ever-so-shaken Graysen muttered to himself, "Time to rent a room!"

# Beware! He Seeks Lost Souls

# (Chapter 4)

A quaint, ivy-covered cottage on the outskirts of town appeared in the offing. Graysen stopped and inquired about it. After inspecting it and the grounds, he decided to make it his new home.

Graysen's new homestead, a quaint cottage, sat nestled in the secrets carried by the town's winds and surrounded by age-old oaks and gnarled elms. Tendrils of ivy clinging to the weathered exterior as if reluctant to let go. The ivy, a tapestry of emerald and shadow, concealed the cottage from prying eyes, casting it in perpetual twilight.

Around the back of the house, the rear porch, a relic from a bygone era, sagged under the weight of memories. Its wooden planks creaked in protest as people stepped onto its uneven surface. A porch swing with rusted chains rusted and entwined with more ivy swayed gently in the breeze. Those who dared to sit there claimed they heard faint echoes of forgotten conversations carried by the wind.

Beyond the rear porch, a seasonal victory vegetable garden flourished. Rows of mustard greens, peas, peppers, plump pumpkins, and fragrant herbs stretched toward the sun. The soil, rich and dark, yielded its bounty with pride. Locals said the carrots tasted sweeter here, and the zucchinis grew to improbable sizes.

Inside, the cottage held an enchanting ambiance. The cozy interior welcomed weary souls seeking refuge from the outside world. The floorboards, polished by generations of footsteps, emitted a soft hum—a lullaby for lost dreams. The walls bore witness to countless winters. The plaster walls adorned with the typical reddish-brown color of old photographs and antique mirrors that reflected more than mere images.

An ancient fireplace served as the focal point of the living room.  Its hearth is wide enough to cradle a dozen stories. The flames danced with a life of their own.  Above the mantel hung a tarnished brass key that no one dared touch.  The realtor said it unlocked hidden chambers within the cottage, while others believed it led to forgotten realms.

The cozy and cluttered kitchen boasted a cast-iron stove that exhaled warmth and memories. Jars of pickled cucumbers and raspberry jam lined the shelves, their handwritten labels fading with time. A wooden table, scarred by knife marks and laughter, stood near the window. Here, the cottage's inhabitants gathered for hearty meals and shared confidences in muted tones.

Upstairs, the bedroom held a four-poster bed draped in faded lace. Moonlight filtered through the curtains, illuminating a worn quilt stitched with love and loss. The closet harbored moth-eaten coats and dresses, each with a story etched into its fabric. The attic, accessible only by a narrow staircase, guarded forgotten trunks and dusty volumes—an archive of secrets waiting to be unraveled.

And so, the quaint cottage stood—a sanctuary for those who sought solace, a keeper of mysteries, and a silent witness to the ebb and flow of time. Its ivy-clad walls whispered tales of love, betrayal, and redemption, carried on the wind to the ancient oaks and gnarled elms that guarded its secrets.

In a place where legends intertwined with reality, this cottage remained an invitation to those who dared to listen, dream, and believe in the magic that defied the ticking clock of the modern world.

From the moment he arrived in Sleepy Hollow, though, he felt restless. Why restless? He shook it off as he could not explain it. What he really felt was excitement! He was here!!! Here, in Sleepy Hollow, he would now live his dream as the new reporter for The Sleepy Hallow Gazette!!! No! No room for restlessness. No, not for him.

While settling into his new home, he remembered that legends always seem to come alive at night. Chuckling, he said, "And now these legends of ghosts and ghouls that haunt the night are playing on my mind!"

He continued to chuckle as he nostalgically remembered his student days when he spent hours in the library. He read multitudes of books with a fascination for dark and mysterious tales. Trying to understand the brooding, foreboding feel, he always held a fascination for the legend where the Headless Horseman, a fearsome figure in a black cloak, reputedly haunted the night.

Now, as a trained paranormal investigator and the newly hired newspaper reporter, he had the golden opportunity to explore the Horseman's grave at the old cemetery. If any paranormal activity exists there, hopefully, he can capture some evidence.

Despite his bright future, he

wondered what lurked in the shadows, the hidden side of Sleepy Hollow. Questioning his judgment, he wondered if he made a mistake moving here.

As he mentally reviewed the pros and cons of accepting such an undertaking, he heard howls in the distance, rustling in the brush, and creaking in his floorboards. While unpacking his paranormal meter and other electronic equipment, he felt the presence of someone or something following him as if they were lying in wait for him. Eerie and unsettling feelings began to get stronger. When he peered out his window, he saw the moon casting a pale light and then noticed long shadows. Upon taking a closer look, he noticed a strange glow, an unusual radiance flickering and dancing in the shadows.

As his apprehension and ominous feelings intensify, he also mused about an old line, "As the moon bathes the town, an eerie glow tends to surface."

Shuddering, Graysen dismissed his

shivers with a quip, "Okay! Time to find the cottage's heater," and off he scurried to start his hunt for it.

As he fidgeted and fumbled through his new lodging, all of a sudden, he heard the sound of distant hoofbeats and caught a glimpse of fleeting and flickering shadows moving amidst the trees.

With a sense of resignation, Graysen decided to take a break! It's been a long, exhausting day. As a matter of fact, it's been a bone-weary dead tired dog day! Continuing to unpack tomorrow sounded like a great idea. Tomorrow, he could also spend time immersing himself in the town's rich history. Spending hours at the local library sounded like a fantastic plan, a fantasy realized. Yes, an absolute dream come true! He could see himself spending hours pouring over worn and weathered manuscripts.

As he stretched out on the sofa, his reeling mind kept swirling. He desperately needed to start an abbreviated form of meditation. Collecting and organizing his jumbled thoughts became easier as he focused on regulating his breathing and clearing his mind.

The day's events left him shaken, and he couldn't shake off the unsettling feelings that lingered after the day's events.

The legend of the Headless Horseman consumed his most pressing thoughts. His convictions that the tale was not a mere folktale, but a part of the town's essence grew as the day wore on. The unacknowledged influence of the Beekman Circle permeated the town's overall story with a sense of reality that he could not ignore. Also, the continued threat of encountering the Horseman was ever-present. Therefore, he knew it all required thorough investigation and documentation.

After giving his body one last head-to-toe stretch, peacefulness washed over him, causing his muscles to relax and his mind to open up to matters that required immediate attention. With each passing moment, he felt his muscles loosen further, and tranquility finally enveloped him.

While mentally setting a more organized schedule for tomorrow, he began to allow his mind to paint a picture of his first autumn evening in Sleepy Hollow.

As he relaxed, he thoroughly relished the rich tapestry of mental images filling his mind.

Suddenly, his peaceful state shattered as he heard a strange whistle in the offing. The intensely unsettling sound came from deep in the densely wooded area outside his window. Unmistakably, it was a man who whistled, followed by the resounding stomp of a stallion. Graysen wondered seriously, "Is there a horse trail out back?"

He unexpectedly encountered a mysterious figure while strolling through a secluded forest path. The stranger dressed in old, dreary clothing held a glint of madness in his eyes as he whispered, "Young traveler, beware of the Horseman! He seeks the lost souls who dare to uncover his secrets." With that, the antiquated man disappeared into the darkness of the night.

Shaken by this attempt to intimidate him made Graysen more driven and determined to uncover the truth behind this menacing greeting. He ventured further into the forest, following the supposed path of the phantom Horseman. As he did so, he unearthed a hidden cemetery.

The gravestones bore numerous inscriptions of names, and each one told the story of a life that once lived. As he forged onward, he stumbled and lost his balance. Facing him stood some more 18th-century headstones. As he grappled with the brush to straighten himself up, he squinted to read the inscriptions on these tombstones. Gasping from shock, he read the names Ichabod Crane and Katrina Van Tassel. Yes, the names of the fabled characters in the legend, shockingly, were now clearly staring right back at him! Jolted by what he read, he felt shivers racing throughout his body.

He could even feel his entire physical form rattle with fright.

Befuddled and perplexed, he stood there paralyzed by the sight and grew physically colder with each passing moment.

Despite the fog, the moon lit the sky well enough. His eyes felt pained by it as its strength illuminated the surrounding soul-stirring graveyard sights, breathing life into its every detail.

As he continued to quake with fear and make sense of the full scope of this cemetery, Graysen found himself facing the bridge where Ichabod Crane's tragic fate unfolded. The sensation of cold that enveloped him made him fear that he was going to die from hypothermia. Feeling his blood drain and then becoming faint, he caught sight of a spectral figure drawing near. The noble rider proudly sat atop a black steed.

Watching what unfolded before his eyes, he physically became immobilized by gripping fear. Graysen realized that the petrifying figure held a pumpkin-like head in his hand.

Unable to speak, Graysen's whole body just continued to tremble and grow limp as he felt a death-like presence brush by him and slink into the darkness.

Panting and in a state of panic, it indeed was as if the legend had come to life before his eyes...but...wait...his hand, yes, his hand was now slapping the side of the sofa...the sofa?...what sofa?...yes, the sofa, his sofa...feeling shock waves run through his body, his eyes popped open. Visually surveying the area, he sighed with a massive amount of relief as he realized it was a dream.

Yes, nothing more than a dream! Or was it a precognitive nightmare foretelling him of what's to come?

The night is dark and cold
A biting chill is in the air
The woods are deep and silent
The eerie silence broken only by the sound of
rustling leaves

The moon is pale and old
And casts a ghostly glow
On the bridge where legends told
Of a headless horseman's fright

He rides along the hollow
With a pumpkin in his hand
Searching for the one to follow
To the realm of shadowland

He seeks the one who killed him
In a bloody battlefield
And took away his freedom
And his helmet and his shield

He roams the night in anger
And in sorrow and in pain
And woe to any stranger
Who dares to cross his lane

For he will chase and haunt them
With his dreadful steed and blade
And he will not relent until
His vengeance is repaid

# Buried Within

# The Whistling Winds

# (Chapter 5)

With dawn breaking, the gentle rays of sunlight pierced through the misty woods. Graysen set about brewing himself a strong cup of espresso and savored the rich aroma of the dark roast. The scent of the morning dew that lingered in the air added a subtle yet refreshing layer to his early morning experience. As he wrapped himself in the warmth and comfort of his new cozy kitchen, Graysen kept shaking his head as he mentally replayed last night's fiendishly demonic dream.

He tried to make sense of his bizarre dream as he slowly moved about his new quarters. Relying on his past studies, Graysen remembered that dreams manifest one's past experiences, present mindset, and future possibilities. The theories surrounding dreams are complex and delve into the intricate workings of the mind, unraveling the mysterious ways in which it interprets and manifests information. Graysen wondered what could have caused his mind to evoke such dark and anxiety-driven dreams. Suddenly, he recalled that unsettling nightmares often arise from unfinished business.

With a deep sense of self-satisfaction, Graysen released a warm and comforting sigh of contentment, feeling at peace with the world. Given that explanation made sense, he leaned back in his kitchen chair and stretched his legs. As he lifted the mug of freshly prepared coffee, he enjoyed inhaling its rich, earthy aroma before drinking it. He then closed his eyes as he slowly took a sip.

His moment of finding peace was short-lived. With an angry force, intense howling like a banshee's scream began, and then whistling winds slammed his kitchen shutters shut with a loud bang. Startled, his arm jerked and swung with such force that his coffee flew in the air.

Physically, his entire body was thrown off balance and knocked sideways in his chair. Outside, he saw dark clouds swirling in the sky. The tree branches creaked and cracked, bending, and swaying like enraged snakes, warning him of something dangerous. Was a menacing storm like a hurricane gathering force? Or something worse?!?

Sensing an unnatural presence, though, he broke out into a cold sweat. His skin prickled with goosebumps and his hair stood on end. Without warning, a low, throaty, unexpected male voice being carried through the strong whistling wind whispered, "Beware, young traveler, he seeks the lost souls who dare to uncover his secrets!" Then, a continuous hiss just ran through the howling wind. Someone, something was watching him and waiting to pounce!

Graysen clutched his heart and made his way to the sofa, feeling like he was about to have a heart attack. His chest tightened and his breath became shallow. Sharp pains shot through his body.

He realized then that his nightmare last night was not just a dream but a prophetic warning. It's all true, he thought. The spirit world showed him the future. He actually had glimpsed the horror that awaited him. He was now thoroughly terrified, his palms truly covered with sweat. His mind, now in a state of chaos, kept thinking, "This voice! That same voice spoke to me in last night's dream. It was a warning! The antiquated man in the woods! My dream is a premonition!!! Oh My God!" Overcome with a sense of dread, he felt a surge of panic and a gripping seizure rising! Fighting the urge to scream, he attempted to regain control over his building hysteria by practicing some regulated and meditative breathing.

After steadying himself by lying on the sofa to start the meditative practice of slowly inhaling and deeply exhaling for about 15 minutes, he sufficiently relaxed his body and mind. Having released all of the gripping tension and stress from his body and mind, he felt calm enough to get up to do some in-depth research about the vast field of dreams.

He walked over to his laptop, sat down, and started clicking away at the keys. The return information struck him like a thunderbolt!

A summary of a Google search said dreams can show us what we are meant to do. Yes! The long list of entries revealed that dreams are a fascinating and mysterious phenomenon that sometimes offers a peek into alternative dimensions, parallel realities, spiritual realms, and even past lives and future possibilities. Dreams are a window into the unknown, where the boundaries of time, space, and logic are blurred, and anything becomes possible.

Anxious to collect more detailed information, he typed: "Can a premonition ever manifest as a precognitive dream?" into Microsoft Edge's browser.

Edge's response to his query was:

A premonition is a feeling or sense of something that is going to happen, while a precognitive dream is a dream that shows a future event or situation 1. Some people believe that premonitions can manifest as precognitive dreams, meaning that they have dreams that accurately predict the future 2.

Very little scientific evidence supports this claim. It is possible that these dreams are just coincidences or influenced by existing knowledge 1. Some historical events, such as Abraham Lincoln's assassination, were reportedly foreseen in dreams, but there is no way to verify the authenticity or accuracy of these accounts 2.

Therefore, the answer to your question depends on your personal beliefs and experiences. Some people may have faith in their intuition and dreams, while others may be more skeptical and rational.

1: Precognitive Dreams, Premonitions and Déjà vu

2: When Our Dreams Feel Like Warnings | Psychology Today

By the time he finished his preliminary exploration into the realm of dreams through both the Google and Edge search engines, he knew that he was onto something big.  He would not let the ominous warning from his precognitive nightmare deter him from his journalistic duty.

His passion for exploring this fascinating horror story grew stronger after reading numerous internet posts. With a newfound sense of determination, he found himself feeling renewed.  Yes, Graysen would now pursue his mission with vengeance.  With his heart, soul, and mind, once again, he cemented his conviction to unveil the hidden secrets lurking in the depths of Sleepy Hollow as they now were intricately intertwined with his destiny.

Feeling satisfied with his reasoning and renewed plans to expose the truth about the Headless Horseman and the dark secrets hidden in the shadows of this town, Graysen went back to his espresso machine to enjoy a fresh cup.

# A Crimson Glow

## (Chapter 6)

"Well, look at that!" exclaimed Graysen. On the horizon, a rare and spectacular crimson glory created by a Blood Moon and Hunter Moon will fill the night sky and nestle within nature's loving embrace on Halloween. With the trees and leaves rustling in the wind, their colors will stupendously blend with the fiery hues of this celestial spectacle. Transfixed by the sheer beauty of the night sky ablaze with such a rare and wondrous sight, it will be a moment that will seem to last forever. A vision so enchanting that townspeople could gaze upon it for hours without ever growing tired of its breathtaking beauty. A moment of pure magic.

Feeling a rush of adrenaline, Graysen started pulling out and looking into his voluminous research material for his feature story about the upcoming lunar eclipse. He wanted to capture its beauty and mystery in his article. "What a mesmerizing vision it will be to see!" He could already picture the awe-inspiring scene.

He found a spellbinding article on the phases of a lunar eclipse with a notation that every eclipse is unique. Yes, no two eclipses are identical! The article explains how these celestial events occur and what causes the hypnotic "Blood Moon" phenomenon. It dives straight into the world of astronomy and explores the captivating wonders of the night sky.

"Oh, what a vision it will be to see!" muttered Graysen as his mind filled with anticipation, vividly imagining the awe-inspiring scene to come. "Such a haunting and chilling spectacle, a deep red moon casting a crimson glow over the town. Imagine the breathtaking extravaganza created by this unique phenomenon looming above the town, distinctively piercing through the darkness of the night. It will be a sight that will leave an indelible mark on the memory of all those fortunate enough to witness it."

Spellbound in thought by the

atmospheric changes about to come, he felt inspired to memorialize this new phase in his life. With pen in hand, he set out to craft his inaugural piece for the Gazette, delving into the subject of the Blood Moon. There is much to say about this celestial event. Despite the red or ruddy brown colored moon having no astronomical significance, it is a sight worth beholding and deserves front-page coverage.

He stretched his body from head to toe and thought, time for some exercise, time to break a sweat. So, he made his list of things to do, like walk into town, run errands, and lunar eclipse research at the local library. Hopefully, they will have an extensive collection of old manuscripts, maps, and maybe even some archaic astronomy equipment.

As he prepared for his trip to the library, Graysen's thoughts turned to the myths and legends surrounding the Blood Moon. He made a mental note to check what legends and myths are associated with the Blood Moon. What could be the truth to them, or if they were simply the manifestation of human imagination and fear.

Scratching his head and tapping his forehead with his index finger, trying to recall any relevant full moon legends, Graysen remembered that some cultures and religions have associated the Blood Moon with various prophecies, omens, or supernatural events.

In Sleepy Hollow, there is a legend that a Blood Moon can resurrect a powerful witch who was burned at the stake in the 18th century. The witch, named Serilda, seeks revenge on the descendants of those who condemned her and leaves a trail of charred corpses in her wake.

Serilda, herself, was a Greek witch and the High Priestess of the Order of the Blood Moon, a dark coven that served Moloch, god of the underworld. She worked alongside the Headless Horseman's Hessian soldiers in the Revolutionary War. She used her dark magic to burn and slaughter the American troops. She was captured and burned at the stake by the magistrate of Sleepy Hollow after the coven of good witches weakened her powers. Before she died, she swore to return and take the flesh of the descendants of those who killed her.

The Order of the Blood Moon is a secret society of witches that has existed in Sleepy Hollow for centuries. The Order has a long history of conflict with the lineage of chosen warriors known as the Witnesses of Sleepy Hollow, as they are destined to stop Moloch.

Responsible for many supernatural events and crimes that plague Sleepy Hollow, The Order uses dark magic, blood rituals, and ancient artifacts to summon and control various creatures and forces of evil. They also have infiltrated multiple institutions and organizations in Sleepy Hollow to target and manipulate innocent people to serve their purposes.

This Order is not only a threat to Sleepy Hollow but to the whole world, with its involvement in global conspiracies that involve other cults, secret societies, and paranormal entities.

Their master plan is to open the gates of hell for Moloch and his army of evil. Only the Witnesses of Sleepy Hollow and their allies can stop them and save the world from the impending doom.

WOW, what a story to research and develop! With that, Graysen stepped out of his cottage and left his home to step into the library's hallowed halls to seek not only dusty tomes but also the echoes of celestial lore.

# The Past Is Not Dead!

## (Chapter 7)

In the shadowed heart of Sleepy Hollow, where the veil between the corporeal and the spectral wavered like a moth's fragile wing, Graysen felt the chill of autumn slither through his coat. The dampness clung to him and seeped into his bones. As he navigated the cobblestone streets with his errands in hand, he thought about how Sleepy Hollow's cobblestones bear witness to more than mere footsteps— they cradle the echoes of forgotten souls.

While "The Legend of Sleepy Hollow" bore a name whispered like a curse through the centuries, Sleepy Hollow, an otherworldly enclave, seemingly wore its secrets like a tattered shroud. The gloomy sky pressed down upon the crooked rooftops, as if the heavens themselves harbored age-old grievances. Laughingly, Graysen noticed his breath materialized in the air, a ghostly echo of his own unease. When he moved to Sleepy Hollow, he expected the quaintness. He even anticipated a touch of eerie nostalgia, the kind that whispered of headless specters galloping through moonlit glades. Sleepy Hollow was more than folklore; it was a living mystery, a wound in time that refused to heal.

The Town Center's clock now loomed before him. It was somewhat obscured by the ominous form of an oversized Jack O'Lantern whose grin stretched wide and whose jagged teeth displayed malevolent intentions. Jack, the pumpkin's nickname, cast menacing shadows on the cobblestones below. Graysen's pulse always quickened when he saw it. To him, Jack was no mere decoration; it was a sentinel, a warden of secrets. Even the townsfolk averted their eyes, as if they sensed the unseen supernatural forces were at play.

Graysen's intrepid journalistic instincts kicked in. While he moved here to unravel the Headless Horseman's tale, he now understood that the legend is but a veil. Beneath it lay a darkness, a whispered pact with the night itself. Jack represents more than festive ornamentation; it's a warning, a beacon for those who dared to pry too deeply.

As he stepped closer, Jack's leering face filled his vision. Jack's hollow eyes seemed to mock him, too, promising peril to his queries. Graysen's fingers brushed Jack's rough form.  He swore he felt an unnatural pulsating sensation as if the very essence of Sleepy Hollow pulsed within Jack's lumpy form.

"There's nothing crisp and refreshing about this day," he murmured, his breath lost in the autumn mistiness, and Jack swung slightly as if nodding in agreement. Graysen's resolve hardened. He would delve deeper and unravel the threads that bound this cursed town. For beyond the legend, beyond the Headless Horseman, lay a conspiracy woven into the very fabric of reality. And Graysen, with ink-stained fingers and an unyielding heart, would be its chronicler even if it meant confronting the looming danger hinted within every shadow.

As he stumbled upon a group of screaming friends running from the cemetery attached to the Old Dutch Church, the winds also picked up their strength. They clawed at his skin, insistent and malevolent. Within them, Graysen clearly heard a voice so low it seemed to rise from the very earth itself, "Beware, for the past is not dead. It is merely dormant."

Caught off guard by the screaming friends on the run from an unseen force and the sudden intensity of the howling winds bearing a perturbingly dark message, Graysen wondered, "Whoa, whose spiritual slumber has been disturbed? Whose buried secrets lying beneath these brittle fallen leaves have been stirred?" The legends spoke of a Headless Horseman, a phantom rider who galloped through the moon-drenched woods, seeking vengeance. But legends were like mist, elusive, ever shifting. What truths truly lay hidden beneath these leaves?

From what Graysen could surmise,

the screeching trio, desperate and wide-
eyed, apparently took advantage of the
Halloween season to visit the Old Dutch
Church's cemetery, where the legend of
the Headless Horseman was born.
Perhaps they hoped to glimpse the
ethereal steed, the one who haunted
Sleepy Hollow's moonlit lanes, its hooves
pounding the earth, its headless form
wreathed in fog.

October generally made the public
think more of Sleepy Hollow as a popular
tourist spot. A place to spend some time
picnicking, historical sightseeing, and
walking about to the different specialty
shops.

Graysen's gaze swept the graveyard.
The tombstones leaned; their inscriptions
weathered by time. Names forgotten;
stories lost. Yet the air crackled with
anticipation. The Sleepy Hollow Horror
Stories shopkeeper who had welcomed
Graysen on his first day had hinted at
more. "Stay awhile," the shopkeeper had
murmured, eyes like ancient mirrors.
"Immerse yourself." These young people

should pitch a tent and stay until they steep themselves in every Sleepy Hollow novelty shop.

They seemingly parked their car near the church entrance and walked along the gravel path, perhaps to tread where shadows clung. As they passed the ancient tombstones and monuments, they could see the granite faces etched with sorrow. Graysen's breath misted in the chilly air so, he thought today's chill probably intensified the dread in their hearts as The Legend, coupled with the dreary, gloomy October weather, usually did that to most people, even if they didn't fully believe the story. They probably also wondered if they were safe in this desolate spot or if someone or something paranormal was watching them.

The wind continued to howl a chorus of forgotten voices. The church bell tolled, its iron tongue resonating through the ages. Graysen stepped forward, drawn toward the heart of this mystery. And as the sky darkened, he vowed to uncover Sleepy Hollow's secrets.

For in Sleepy Hollow, the past laid like a slumbering beast waiting to awaken, and Graysen would be its scribe.

Graysen stood at the edge of the clearing, his breath still a ghostly plume in the misty air. The band of young people looked like shadows themselves and seemed to move like wraiths, their faces half-hidden by fear or perhaps something more insidious.

While he couldn't clearly see the trio; they seemed to run from a clearing where they happened to come across a strange sight.

Taking a walk over to the site that they just ran from, he found lying on the grass the remnants of their hurried departure. A gnarled walking stick, its wood twisted like aged bones; an ugly sweater, its yarn unraveling; and an abandoned wicker picnic basket, its woven fibers still warm from handling. It made him wonder what could've driven them to leave in such a rush, abandoning their belongings as if they were mere trifles.

The sweater bore fall leaves and a pumpkin design. Who'd wear such a thing to a gravestone rubbing tour? Graysen shivered as his fingers brushed the fabric and he smelled its aroma. This sweater held memories of crisp apples and crackling leaves, of harvest moons and whispered promises.

As Graysen held the walking stick in his hands, he couldn't help but notice the intricate carvings on its surface. The symbols etched onto the wood seemed to have been created by a skilled but still trembling hand. The engravings also spoke of forgotten rituals and ancient knowledge. He wondered whose gnarled and weathered fingers had shaped it and what kind of spiritual protection was invoked. Perhaps, something darker, something more underworld. The walking stick seemed to hold many secrets and mysteries, and Graysen couldn't help but feel drawn to its ancient power.

Their feast laid bare in the picnic

basket. Sandwiches with crusts untouched. In season apples with their skins taut creating the impression they were preserving secrets within. The thermos, a vessel of warmth for the autumn season, filled with a fragrant pumpkin spice latte.

"Something scared them!" he declared. "Something spooky, something creepy. It made them run away...run for their lives!!!"

Graysen's gaze swept the clearing again. "From what, though?" he wondered, nervously glancing around. "What were they running from?"

And then, in a sarcastic twist, he thought, "The Headless Horseman, perhaps?" The words hung in his mind like cobwebs, but it would be silly to take that thought seriously. It's too early in the day for such tales to come alive.

Despite the seemingly soundness of his analysis, Graysen held onto that thought. The Headless Horseman is a specter woven into the very fabric of this cursed place. Ghostly hooves thundered through the ages, seeking retribution. And as the wind stirred the fallen leaves, in Sleepy Hollow, shadows danced, and secrets only slumbered as the past was never truly dead. It was merely dormant, waiting for a curious soul to awaken it.

Trying to mask his uneasiness, Graysen chuckled as if to ward off the silence. Noticing a nearby tree, his face grew pale, and his eyes widened. "What's that?" As he walked closer to it, he gasped, and his eyes became riveted on the tree trunk. There was a huge gash on it, as if someone had slashed it with a sharp axe. The wound was fresh, and the sap was oozing out like blood. With his eyes rolling, he wondered "What's with the huge gash?"

He noticed a crude wooden board as he tried to make sense of it all. The letters looked like they were stained with blood. The sign read:

BEWARE
OF THE
HEADLESS
HORSEMAN
HE IS REAL!

Feeling paralyzed and unable to speak, Graysen gawked at the sign in horror. Now, starting to feel like a nervous breakdown was looming, his body began to uncontrollably shake. Fearing someone might be watching him in this isolated part of the woods, he wanted to turn on his heels and ran back to the church!!!

When Graysen watched the trio from a distance, he was puzzled by their behavior. He heard parts of their conversation but didn't believe what he was hearing. He thought they were just playing a prank on each other, or maybe they were high on something. He shrugged off their panic and smirked, "October in Sleepy Hollow! Geez!!!"

Little did he know, his skepticism would soon be challenged as he unknowingly walked into the heart of a real-life horror story. As he stood there, he didn't notice the dark clouds gathering in the sky, or the wind picking up speed. He didn't see the crows circling above him, or the ravens perching on the trees.

He didn't hear the whispers echoing in the air or the laughter mocking him. He didn't feel the presence that was following him or the breath that was on his neck. He didn't know that he actually was his next target.

# Boy Meets Girl

# (Chapter 8)

The air in Sleepy Hollow was filled with the promise of something magical as the scent of vibrant red, orange, and gold autumn leaves danced in the gentle breeze, creating a mesmerizing tapestry against the gray sky. It was as if nature was preparing for a grand spectacle, ready to unveil something transformative. With a heart eager for adventure, Graysen's eyes sparkled with curiosity as he strolled down the historic streets, lined with ancient oaks that whispered tales of the town's mysterious past. He couldn't help but feel a thrilling mix of anticipation and excitement.

Seeking a spot to enjoy a midday meal, he felt a magnetic pull towards a charming boutique tucked away amidst a row of vintage shops. The sign above the entrance proclaimed, "A Magical Getaway." They offered a wide array of magical potions, teas, brews, lotions, trinkets, and other enchanting items and a collection of classic and modern books. Bewitched, he entered.

As he stepped inside, the door emitted a gentle chime. An array of entrancing items, charms, books, and other alluring merchandise spread out before him. The shelves were filled with bottles. The walls were adorned with potions, lotions, and herbs that exuded an invigorating aura. The shop's atmosphere was filled with a delightful blend of fragrances emanating from the various products.

Katherine was engrossed in organizing the shelves of her boutique when the sound of the bell chimed through the air. Her gaze lifted to behold the entrance of a striking gentleman clad in a sleek leather jacket. His hair was a rich shade of dark, his eyes a riveting green, and his smile exuded a certain charm.

A mesmerizing young woman with a celestial aura, Katherine stood still. Her bewitching eyes and entrancing gaze held his. Time seemed to stand still. The spark of chemistry between them was powerful, to say the least. There was an immediate, unspoken connection, a recognition of a wordless bond that went beyond the ordinary. Her mind, spirit, and senses felt good about meeting this newcomer.

Graysen approached her counter, his gaze still locked with Katherine's. "Hello," he said, his voice blending excitement with curiosity. "I'm the new reporter at The Sleepy Hollow Gazette and was looking for a place to lunch. Your boutique's bewitching style is too alluring to ignore, so I decided not to resist the temptation to explore your enchanting store first."

Katherine's smile radiated warmth from within her that seemed to melt away the autumn chill. "Welcome to Sleepy Hollow," she replied, her eyes sparkling with a hint of mischief as she sort of sang. "How can I assist you in finding your own touch of magic today?"

Graysen, spellbound by both the charm of the boutique and the enthralling woman before him, willingly drew himself deeper into their conversation. He was sure that Katherine could share tales of Sleepy Hollow's spiritual, otherworldly history, weaving stories of love, folklore, and the unexplained. Graysen, with his passion for storytelling, prepared himself to hang on to her every word.

As they spoke, it became evident that their worlds were intricately woven together. Graysen's mind headlined the next upcoming Sleepy Hollow Gazette banner as: "Addressing Otherworldly Interests," written by Graysen, the inquisitive reporter with a pen who seeks to uncover truths and assisted by the ever so hypnotic Katherine Vanessa Talisman, proprietor, A Mystical Escape. Fascinated by his desire to delve into the paranormal and deeply discover the spirit world hidden within the town's stories, she, in turn, was a witch in love.

Graysen couldn't help but imagine how his days could seamlessly transform into weeks spent at Katherine's A Mystical Escape shop. He couldn't help but imagine the joy of seeing her regularly, going on dates, and perhaps even... He could envision their plans falling into place, allowing them to discover the town side by side. Unraveling the mysteries together, they forged their own unique tale. He longed for the ultimate fulfillment in life with her by his side. It would be the peak of perfection that he hoped for.

As they talked, they discussed their common interests more deeply. The more they talked, the more he saw Katherine's enchanting boutique as a fiery and passionate backdrop for their blossoming romance. In his mind, he continued to see that each encounter to come would be a collaborative chapter written by them, a storytelling reporter and a Sleepy Hollow enchantress, in a tale that seemed written in the stars of Sleepy Hollow.

He wanted to ensure before he left her shop that when the sun dipped below the horizon, and the town embraced the hush of the night, Graysen would find himself standing before Katherine with one specific question, "Would you like to explore the mysteries of Sleepy Hollow together as partners in our own adventure to identify where reality intertwines with enchantment? I so want to be your companion in our very own extraordinary escapade!"

Katherine's eyes kept twinkling with joy as they talked. Her continued nodding during their conversation sealed their fates.

Continually imagining their future unfolding together as they stepped out into the moonlit streets hand in hand, Graysen knew it would feel as though the town itself had conspired to bring two kindred spirits together. Their love story will become another chapter in the rich tapestry of Sleepy Hollow's enchanted history.

By now, they were warmly holding hands. During a lull in their conversation, Katherine mentioned, "I don't serve lunch, but I just made some scrumptious peanut butter bars. Would you like some with tea?" He eagerly nodded, yes!

She walked him over to a cozy corner with a sofa sitting area. She set down the delectable peanut butter bars on the table and went to make some tea.

As she puttered about her shop, he said, "I'm preparing to write a feature on the upcoming Blood Moon, sometimes called The Hunter Moon. I would like to interview you about your witchcraft practices and photograph your shop."

Another surge of that ever-so-delightful electricity seemed to pass between them as she smiled and said, "Wow, that sounds fantastic!" "Yes, yes! Absolutely!!! In addition to the wares on the shelves and strewn throughout the shop, I am also an event planner for escape room parties."

She graciously offered him tea as he asked, "Well, how did you get into this business?"

She told him that she was born in Sleepy Hollow, the place where reality and magic seamlessly co-exist. Like the rest of the town, she, too, always was captivated by the allure of magic and mystery. Fortunately, she inherited the boutique from her grandmother, a witch. Yes, a real live witch! So, her heritage blended beautifully with her entrepreneurial spirit. Moreover, she simply loves crafting innovative products and curating unforgettable customer experiences. And the escape room's business is today's latest craze.

Katherine felt that Graysen listened attentively, nodding, and asking thoughtful follow-up questions. She could tell he was impressed by her passion, creativity, and ingenuity. Their mutual attraction was obviously quite intense. Their human connection? Undeniable.

When he took out his cell and asked if he could photograph her and the shop now, she happily consented and effortlessly struck a pose for him. She tried to look natural and relaxed but couldn't help feeling overly excited. She liked how he looked at her and yearned for it to be permanent.

They spent the next hour talking and laughing as he devoured her peanut butter bars. Graysen intently listened as he wanted to learn more about Katherine's offbeat life and interests. They shared a lot of viewpoints, such as their love for books, movies, and music. Of course, the best part of the conversation was finding out they were both single and contemporaries!

During their conversation, she felt what he felt, a wave of optimism for a deeply meaningful, intimate relationship. When he asked her if she would like to join him for dinner later, she unabashedly showed her happiness and said yes. In her eyes, she could help him learn more about the town, and his visionary mind could help her develop plans for new escape rooms.

Katherine felt a magnificent sense of fluttering in her stomach. She enthusiastically gave him her cell, email, and social media links. Flush with euphoria, she pondered the path that this new partnership would take.

They warmly embraced and shared a goodbye kiss on the cheek.

With a wave, Graysen left the shop with the final words that he would be back for dinner. The warm glow in Katherine's heart turned into burning flames of love as she watched him go. She wanted to close the shop and go home to get ready for their lovely dinner date. She knew that this night was going to be a night to remember.

When Graysen left her shop, he also felt an intense euphoria about them. Laughingly, he wondered what secret ingredients she, his bewitching beloved, his newfound heartthrob, Katherine Vanessa Talisman, put into those peanut butter bars. Hopefully, as the afternoon wore on, they won't prove to be "funny" bars.

As he skipped with delight along the narrow pathway, he suddenly tripped. The afternoon air thickened with an unspoken dread as he lurched forward and fell to the ground. The trees leaned in; the leaves turned down on their branches. A storm seemingly was brewing, but the ground beneath his feet strangely felt as though it pulsed.

As his fall sent him sprawling forward, his hands grazed the cold, damp street. Looking at the ground to see what caused his tumble, he noticed a human skull whose hollow eye sockets were staring at him. With a mix of amusement and disbelief, he laughingly shook his head and somewhat scoffed as he muttered to himself, this town really does go into overkill on this Headless Horseman tale.

Aggravated from losing his balance, he kicked the discarded skull to one side and picked up his pace. Hearing a hiss, he turned and saw a billowing cloud of steam pouring up through a gutter grate. Oddly enough, it's the exact spot where the skull landed. Yes, the skull landed upright on top of the steaming gutter grate. Stunned, he noticed a veil of steam now covering the skull.

Oh well, he might as well embrace this weird coincidence as he now was a resident, someone planting roots to grow a family tree with his Katherine Vanessa

Talisman, the town witch who bears a touch of magic!

He picked up his pace as he thought about what a Halloween celebration this year would be when he and Katherine celebrate it with the townspeople under the full Blood Moon, The Hunter Moon!

A weak cry pierced the flow of his thoughts, though. The almost inaudible whimper also caused him to somewhat turn his head back. The discarded skull, now encased in steam flowing up through the gutter grate, was still within his sight. With a sense of panic, he wondered, "Wait! What was that? Where did that faint cry come from?" He didn't have time to investigate this eerie cry. He had no choice; he was out of discretionary time. He needed to get on with his errands and quicken his speed. Time was slipping away.

As he accepted his quandary and moved on, he heard a low-sounding, sadistic laughter. Was the now shrouded-in steam skull freakishly giving off these sounds? Or did some unseen prankster seize the opportunity to take advantage of this Halloween-ish phenomenon?

# A Mystical Escape

## (Chapter 9)

Katherine's face lit up with joy, and she simply couldn't contain her excitement as she eagerly prepared for the upcoming evening. As the afternoon wore on, she continued to reflect on her dreamboat, the man who just stole her heart as he fidgeted with his cell and nervously worked to pursue a conversation just to spend more time with her. Katherine knew from his talk that this New York City boy was used to something other than small-town living. She promised herself to make their dinner date a memorable first night for him with her.

She rolled around various thoughts, thinking, "Are you ready for the adventure of a lifetime?" She envisioned holding his hand as she led him through an exciting evening of twists and turns. She could see him nodding and trying to act confident. Saying things like, "Sure, why not? What do you have in mind?" She would lean closer to his ear and whisper, "Follow me."

She considered leading him to the dark alley behind her boutique. She would point to the door where the sign read "A Mystical Escape." After opening the door, she would gesture for him to enter.

Hopefully, he would look at her with hesitancy, curiosity, and apprehension and finally ask, "What is this place?"

She needed to think of an innovative way to officially introduce him to all aspects of her business. When he asked how it works, she wanted to give him detailed explanations that left him bewitched. She wanted him to become so entranced that he would never want to leave her company,

So, she toyed with the explanation in her mind. "I create immersive escape rooms for thrill-seekers and those who crave challenge. It's an exhilarating and fulfilling experience unlike any other games out there. Much more exciting and rewarding than common games!"

She continued to explain, "You choose from a range of themes like horror, mystery, fantasy, or sci-fi. After you step inside, you find yourself in a captivating room filled with intriguing puzzles and hidden clues. Make sure you solve them within an hour. If you achieve your goal, you will be rewarded with a prize. If you fail, you'll find yourself in a situation where you must wait until someone else comes to your rescue."

As she mentally replayed her explanation, she wondered if he would frown. Would he say something like, "That sounds…creepy!!!"

She laughed softly to herself and thought about how she would reassure him. Say something like, "Don't worry, it's not creepy. It's actually amusing and thrilling. By tapping into your imagination and ingenuity, you can conquer challenges, evade peril, and escape danger. It feels like you are entering a vividly imagined world where every detail comes to life. It's like being in a movie or a book."

Would he doubt her word?

What about if he asks about the cost? Should she say, "It depends on the theme and the difficulty level. But trust me, it's worth it."

What if he sighed and said, "I don't know… I'm not really into this kind of thing." Should she pout? Should she plead ever so slightly? "Please? Just give it a try for me. I really want to show you what I do."

Would he look into her eyes and see sincerity and excitement in them. Or would she be inducing a pang of guilt for rejecting her offer?

"Okay!!!" she said with a nonchalant shrug. These are her considerations for this evening's event and conversation.

She excitedly clapped her hands. The thoughts of bringing him, her newfound soulmate, inside her Mystical Escape room and her life made her feel an overwhelming sense of euphoria. It was as if the universe had aligned, serenading her with a harmonious melody that she hoped would soon become their shared song.

Since he loved The Legend of Sleepy Hollow, should she suggest their first theme be gothic horror?

Standing over an incense dish and inhaling its powerful and soothing scent, Katherine thought that, like a silent language, speaking feelings without words, she would spend the rest of the afternoon working on crafting an indelible vibe. With every detail meticulously chosen and every element perfectly placed, Katherine's unforgettable vibe would transport them to a world of magic and enchantment. Her efforts would evoke a vibrant and colorful halo around them. The town's newly minted couple would encapsulate the essence of Sleepy Hollow.

Katherine Vanessa Talisman stood in the heart of her quaint boutique. Her shop, a haven of ancient wisdom, is a treasure trove of knowledge, featuring books that hold tales of enchantment and long-lost myths within its pages. Shelves are filled with incantations, aromatic teas, and cherished recipes lovingly passed down through countless generations of her family.

Inhaling deeply, she closes her eyes and begins to tap into her inner spirit, channeling the energy of her ancestors and the centuries of wisdom that fill her store.

Ancient wisdom teaches that burning incense is a powerful way to arouse a desire for love. The potency of the ritual is enhanced when a witch chants or sings a love song while gracefully waving her hands over the swirling smoke to direct its energy. By visualizing two lovers deeply and passionately looking into each other's eyes, their connection intensifies, enhancing the power of the incantation in a powerful love ritual. The blend of sensory experiences in this ritual creates a captivating and precise atmosphere, enhancing the desired emotions and amplifying the potency of the experience.

Now in a trance, Katherine felt the profound sensation of her spirit overtake her body, yes, her entire physical form. Breathing in the potent blend of incense, Katherine experienced a surge of psychic energy racing through her body. As her spirit form grew more robust, her mystical form filled every inch of her quaint shop's quarters. She, the charmer, felt herself being lifted by an invisible force.

As her solemn witch's incantation began, she heard her voice reaching out to the cosmic realm, with every word ringing like a bell tolling through the universe.

With the enchanting essence of the rose,
I call upon the magic of love from the heavens above.

By the power of the rose, I invoke the force of love
To fill my heart and soul with beauty from above

By the power of lavender, I invoke the force of calm
To soothe my mind and body with peace and healing balm

By the power of sandalwood, I invoke
the force of spirit
To protect me from all harm and purify
my merit

By the power of frankincense, I invoke
the force of wisdom
To enlighten me with faith and connect
me to the kingdom

By the power of myrrh, I invoke the
force of healing
To cleanse me from all negativity and
bring me blessings

By the power of cinnamon, I invoke the
force of passion
To ignite my creativity and energy for
action

By the power of these six, I invoke the
force of magic
To manifest my will and make my love
life complete.

Just as she finished saying those words, her shop's door chimed, and she found herself facing a delivery driver bearing a bouquet of daises.

Without stumbling or faltering, Katherine reached out to graciously accept the bouquet of daisies.

In the language of love, Graysen's first love letter read,

My dearest Katherine,

Your presence shines with the essence of beauty and grace amidst this sleepy town, my new hometown!

I admire your talent and unwavering passion for your craft, how you masterfully create mystical potions, enchanting elixirs, teas, herbs, lotions, soothing balms, and other botanical remedies that heal a person's body and an aching soul. Your sense of adventure and fun challenges the mind and the spirit. You are everything I dreamed of, my inspiration, muse, and friend.

As a gesture of warmth and affection, I hope you will accept this beautiful bouquet of daisies and my invitation to share my new life and journey in Sleepy Hollow.

With dinner before us, I need you to know that you made me the happiest man and newcomer in Sleepy Hollow.

Warmest regards,

After reading Graysen's love letter, she immediately lit some incense sticks. In typical Sleepy Hollow tradition, she positioned them in her shop's window as a subtle yet unmistakable signal of her interest in him.

Historically, young couples often engaged in a romantic ritual of lighting incense sticks and placing them in their windows to express their burning desire for each other. The thin tendrils of smoke that wafted from the smoldering incense would serve as a powerful signal of their passion. Any potential suitors passing by could see this open display of affection from a distance. This discreet yet captivating romantic practice added a touch of magic and mystery to the art of courtship. It's still a cherished tradition today. Cherished in Sleepy Hollow, NY, that is.

By the time Graysen returned for dinner, the air was thick with the heady scent of love.

When the boutique door chimed, the enchantress Katherine Vanessa Talisman conjured up and unleashed the mystical powers of love with one final majestic swirl.

The mysticism she stirred and infused into her boutique's air began to pulsate with an otherworldly energy. Soft candlelight flickered, casting dancing shadows on the walls adorned with tapestries depicting mythical creatures. The air was rich with the heady scent of incense, a blend of rose, lavender, sandalwood, frankincense, myrrh, and cinnamon. Soft music played in the background, filling the space with a melodic enchantment. The lush carpet beneath her feet cushioned each step as Katherine gracefully glided through her shop. The delicate touch of crystal vials added an extra layer of excitement to her every move. The atmosphere in her shop, A Magical Escape, was now alive and brimming with the enchantment of her age-old magic.

This magical escape and its ethereal atmosphere marked a place where dreams come true, and love fills the air being breathed by the beings of those who stand within it. This spellbound spot, magically marked with an X, marked the new chapter in the lives of Katherine and Graysen.

Katherine and Graysen were locked in a lover's embrace before the door closed. Instead of kissing him, though, she found herself quizzically asking. "What was that sadistic laugh I just heard?"

As Graysen tightened his lover's embrace on Katherine, his facial expression changed to worrisome, and he said in a low, "I don't know. I heard it early this afternoon, though."

Completely flabbergasted, the now stunned Katherine incredulously asked, "What?"

# Bewitched By Our Cuisine

## (Chapter 10)

Moving closer to Halloween left the streets of Sleepy Hollow overflowing with pumpkins, scarecrows, and lanterns. Graysen felt good about his new hometown, but he couldn't quite put into words why he still felt a tinge of unease as he strolled with Katherine toward their restaurant, Bewitched By Our Cuisine. Her mysterious aura seemingly embodied him, and he first felt it when they embraced this evening.

Their cozy and charming restaurant specialized in seasonal and local cuisine. The soft glow of candles and twinkling fairy lights created a warm and intimate atmosphere. The welcoming hostess guided them to a table with a beautiful view of the outside. Paintings and photographs of Sleepy Hollow's history and legends adorned the walls. All pictures of the Headless Horseman, Ichabod Crane, and Katrina Van Tassel hung in the most prominent spots.

After they were seated and enjoying some small talk, Graysen unexpectedly and uncontrollably started to tremble. Simultaneously, Katherine seemingly shuddered, too. He could see her visibly shaking in her chair. It was as if a dreaded invisible force had just shot through them with a wave of trepidation. Feeling disoriented and bewildered, he dismissed the experience and turned his attention back to Katrina Van Tassel's portrait.

While she clearly is not a new name in Sleepy Hollow, he never considered discussing her with Katherine Vanessa Talisman this evening, so he continued to dismiss his unease and studied the menu closer.

What a hauntingly diverse array of dishes! Appetizers such as pumpkin soup, roasted chestnuts, and smoked salmon made choosing only one starter plate difficult. The tantalizing aroma of the braised lamb shank, roasted duck, and mushroom risotto caused his taste buds to tingle with anticipation. The apple pie, pumpkin cheesecake, and chocolate cake desserts hit a home run with him.

When he signaled the familiar (witch's helper) that he wanted a drink, Katherine glowed and radiantly smiled at him. His heart skipped a beat. What a wonderful evening it was going to be. "Graysen. You look handsome tonight," she said, to which he responded, "You look beautiful, Katherine." The connection and life force people in love were supposed to feel kept growing and enveloping them in a world of sweet indulgence.

They ordered dinner and started to share their forever alliance by chatting about Graysen's passion for journalism and Katherine's fascination with magic and the spirit world. Savoring the sweetness of the evening, they toasted their shared fate and sipped their witches brew.

After dinner, they slowly traipsed along the river, taking in the serene beauty of the moonlight reflecting off the water. They held hands, but suddenly, both felt a powerful searing of an unimaginable force, like a swarm of tiny needles pricking their skin, coursing through their entire bodies. The sensation was so intense that they were left stunned. Looking to each other for solace, they were left bewildered and unsure of what had happened.

Scared, they stopped at a rickety bridge. Leaning on the railing, they fortified their strength by holding onto each other. With each new wave of terror, they continually pulled each other closer as they felt the swelling and outpouring of their fears. This layer of complexity thrust upon their newfound relationship made them earnestly question the danger and perilous uncertainty of this unsettling moment.

As fear engulfed them, Graysen and Katherine instinctively kept clinging onto each other, seeking comfort and strength in their shared vulnerability. Their hearts pounded in their chests, their breathing quickened, and their minds raced with a mix of fear and determination. At that moment, a profound realization of how much they cared for each other and how they would do whatever it took to protect one another from whatever supernatural force they faced. It was a moment that would forever bind them, their love becoming a shield against the unknown.

They felt trapped, as though they were in a scene out of a gothic horror movie. They shook as the powerful gusts of the winds started and then picked up speed like a gale force. The fallen leaves rose and twirled as though they were under the dreadful influence of an invisible force. As the winds' force grew, it seemed like the withered leaves encircled an unseen spirit, a supernatural presence from the underworld that evoked a sense of impending doom, a violent death. Bewildered by the significance of this ghastly occurrence, Graysen and Katherine wondered what these abnormal ghostly phenomena represented to their gentle, tender, and passionate relationship.

As they tried to talk about this frightening phenomenon unfolding before them, a malevolent man's chilling, demonic laugh loudly echoed through the night air. The deep and dark laughter created a feeling of foreboding as though imminent danger lurked nearby. Stunned and speechless, their terror-filled eyes began to anticipate facing an ominous and evil entity from the very dark, very hellish spirit world.

After the spectral haunting laughter filled the air, the gale force abruptly died. The swirling leaves dropped to the ground with a heavy thud, leaving the shocked young couple speechless.

After Katherine and Graysen returned to her boutique, emotionally exhausted, they settled down in their cozy corner to fan themselves and leisurely sip some calming tea. Though they both seemed eager to discuss their hair-raising experience, they held back, realizing that delving too deep into such a heady conversation might be overwhelming at the moment. They decided to give each other some space, collect their thoughts, and mull over their incomprehensible paranormal experience.

Switching their conversation back to something they wanted to share in their budding relationship, Katherine asked

Graysen if he was ready to see her Mystical Escape room. He energetically welcomed the opportunity to try it out.

Katherine led him out the backdoor of her boutique and into a room with a sign over the doorway that read: A Mystical Escape.

As Graysen slowly pushed the door open, he was immediately hit by a cold, musty air that seemed to emanate from within the dark room. The only light source came from a dimly lit lamp hanging from the ceiling, barely illuminating the space and casting long, eerie shadows on the walls. Chains hung from the ceiling, and the sound of them clinking against each other reverberated through the room, adding to the ominous atmosphere. The walls were splattered with dark, crimson stains that looked like blood, and a pungent smell filled the air. As Graysen stepped forward, he noticed the floor was littered with scattered bones. The unsettling ambiance intensified with each step as the scattered bones on the floor crunched under his feet. The knot in the pit of his stomach intensified as he realized that he was entering a room filled with unknown horrors and challenges that lay ahead.

The aura alone left him with a sense that he would suffer terrifying nightmares. Yes, haunting and bone-chilling nightmares! Crunch, crunch!!! After all, who could stand all this skin-crawling stuff? Whose nerves wouldn't be set on edge given the eerie and unsettling ambiance that completely engulfed a person? The sound of footsteps continually echoing through the darkness is enough to cause a person's heart to race faster than initially thought possible. Look, some sinister artifact smiled wickedly at him, and then, in a flash, a flashlight suddenly starts flashing a light in his face. While still somewhat blinded, out of nowhere, a zombie extended its decaying arm and suggested a handshake. The mere sight of the creature filled Graysen with revulsion.

"Welcome to my horror room," a chilling voice whispered. "Your goal is to find the elusive key that will unlock the exit door on the other side of the room."

Feeling nervous and tense, his eyes darted around the room. "How do I find it?" he asked. A black-gloved hand pointed to a large painting on the wall opposite them. "It's behind that painting," a muffled voice from the shadows said. Graysen cautiously walked towards the painting.

As he got closer, he noticed something strange. The painting seemed to change shape, morph every time he looked at it. He thought his visual distortions couldn't be from a holdover of Katherine's peanut bars. Still, sometimes, it looked like an abstract swirl of colors, sometimes like a realistic portrait of someone. Other times, it looked like nothing at all.

He felt uneasy as he stared at it. "What is this?" he asked Katherine.

She nonchalantly shrugged her shoulders. "It's just an old painting," she said casually, "with some special effects to make it look different depending on how you look at it."

He frowned suspiciously. "Are you sure?" She nodded confidently.

"Of course, I'm sure," she said sweetly. "Why don't you try looking at it from different angles?" He did as she suggested, but nothing changed about the painting except for his perception of it. He felt ill at ease as he continued to look at it, but he decided not to question Katherine further.

He knew she wanted a lifetime relationship with him as he did with her, so he didn't want to upset her or risk ruining their date. So, he turned his attention back to finding the hidden key behind the painting, which was the only way to escape this horror show.

As he politely tried to finish her escape room challenge, he thought that no matter what happened tonight, ignoring the feeling that something was wrong with it was the better course of action. Even though he wasn't impressed with her escape room, he remained fixed in his belief that Katherine Vanessa Talisman would soon become his wife. After searching his soul for words of reassurance, he drew her close and explained that he needed to leave for the evening. However, he wanted to see her at least for lunch tomorrow, preferably for breakfast, too. Those peanut bars were so good!

She let out a hearty laugh and hugged him. He was such a fabulous new dimension in her life. She welcomed him for both breakfast and lunch.

With that green light signal, Graysen opened his heart to her and said, "Now and then, I need to pause, shut my eyes tight, and embrace you tightly, even if it's only in my imagination. It's hard to put into words, but there's something so captivating and awe-inspiring about the power of love. It's the most beautiful thing in the world, and when I think about you, I can't help but feel completely overwhelmed with emotion."

Katherine simultaneously beamed and cried. As he opened her shop's door to go home, he again reminded her that "the most beautiful thing in the world is love! Good night, Katherine. I thoroughly loved our evening together."

# A Blast from the Past

## (Chapter 11)

With his mind still reeling from his declaration of love, he made his way home. Graysen strolled down the quiet street, absorbed in thought about the evening's events. The image of Katherine Vanessa Talisman, his beautiful future wife, occupied his mind, filling him with an overwhelming sense of excitement and joy. He dreamed of the day they would marry and build their life together in the charming town of Sleepy Hollow.

As a writer, Graysen had come to Sleepy Hollow to explore its rich culture, intriguing history, and current events. Being with Katherine reminded him of his fascination with Katrina Van Tassel, the captivating and mysterious woman from Washington Irving's famous story. Graysen was drawn to the legend of Katrina, who enchanted not only Ichabod Crane but many other men. Known for her mesmerizing charm, she ultimately married Brom Bones and appeared to live happily ever after.  Graysen couldn't help but wonder about the hidden depths behind Katrina's role in the story.  Was she really the entrancing woman the legend made her out to be?  He yearned to uncover the reality underneath the myth, to delve deeper into the character that had captured his imagination.

While Graysen's curiosity to learn more about his new home grew, he also discovered that the town was not as sleepy as it seemed.  Strange incidents happened all around.  Animals acted strangely, people disappeared without a trace, and shopkeepers openly participated in creepy and realistic-looking Halloween pranks.  With rumors of ghosts and hauntings widely circulating, the fear factor among tourists grew exponentially.  As Graysen walked home, his nosiness piqued.  He decided to investigate one particular spot before returning home.

He followed a trail of clues that led him to an old mansion on the outskirts of town. The now empty homestead loomed before him, its windows like empty eyes staring into the abyss. He had heard tales and legends passed down from generation to generation in the taverns, but Graysen was a skeptic. A reporter seeking to separate the facts from the long-held fables.

He saw a soft glow emanating from one of the windows. It beckoned him, promising answers. He couldn't resist the temptation to stealthily sneak inside. He pushed the heavy door open and entered, only to find the darkness swallowing him. Graysen's footsteps echoed through the hallway, each step a hesitant beat against the decrepit floorboards. The air clung to him, thick and suffocating. By the moonlight, Graysen could see dust swirling around the remnants of lives long gone. The rooms were a mausoleum of forgotten memories filled with old furniture and paintings. The paintings hung askew, their subjects staring out with hollow eyes. Among the cracked walls and artwork, a come-hither portrait of a young woman with long blonde hair, fractured ice-blue eyes, and a fair complexion hung proudly among the possessions. An elegant pearl necklace adorned her throat, and the fabric on her pristine white dress seemed untouched by time.

As Graysen approached the portrait, he felt a strange connection as if he knew the woman. As his fingers touched the smooth surface of the glass, an electric jolt ran through his body, causing him to gasp and pull his hand back. He felt as though the world shifted.

Suddenly, a voice behind him softly cooed, "Hello, Graysen."

Electricity surged through him. He knew her, not from this life, but from somewhere deeper, a place where souls danced on the edge of eternity. Her name was Katrina Van Tassel.

He turned around, and there she stood, a mysterious figure representing the woman in the portrait. He couldn't see her face, though. It was obscured, veiled in darkness. The figure spoke, and her wafting voice seemed to carry an otherworldly quality to its chilling tone when she said, "I've been eagerly awaiting your return since you were 10 and first visited Sleepy Hollow."

Graysen mind raced. He realized that the form represented Katrina Van Tassel, but her actual appearance markedly differed. She appeared evil, and he speculated that death must change a person.

As panic clawed at his chest, he tried to flee and run. Unfortunately, an icy wind froze him in place. His limbs literally would not move.

The woman's sinister voice grew fiercer, more intense, and resolute as she declared, "I'm going to make you mine!"

Desperation consumed him as her eyes bore into his soul.

Graysen's heart raced, his breath quickened, and a wave of terror washed over him as he anxiously searched for an escape from the ghostly force that had ensnared him.

As he--and--the room seemed to tremble, a deeper, more malevolent voice said, "Graysen, you've trespassed where mortals dare not tread. Now, your fate is sealed!"

He felt the ghostly force tightened its grip, and then his vision blurred. He glimpsed the woman's face, twisted by sorrow and hunger. Death indeed changed her. But what awaited him in this war between reality and the supernatural worlds? Graysen wondered if separating fact from fiction was a luxury he could no longer afford.

His body was getting ready to instinctively react to these threats when out of the blue, a deep, dark, menacing laugh echoed through the desolate mansion. Graysen fainted.

# What Was That!?!

## (Chapter 12)

As Graysen slowly regained consciousness, he heard a deep, devilishly wicked chortle ringing in his ears and echoing throughout the forsaken mansion. Yes, a cruel and maniacal cackle that seemed to come from the depths of hell even reverberated in the empty halls of the deserted Van Tassel homestead. The entire tone of this paranormal experience seemed infused with malice and malevolence. The now jittery Graysen felt swallowed up within its foreboding and perilous atmosphere.

Struggling to open his eyes, he felt disoriented and feeble, like he was pinned to the floor by an invisible force. Unfortunately, his lack of physical strength held him down on the floor. His limbs felt heavy and uncooperative, making each movement painful and exhausting. It took every ounce of strength he had left to crawl towards the nearby chair, his muscles screaming in protest with each inch he moved.

When he reached the chair, he gripped its legs, painstakingly clawed, and dragged himself up. He leaned heavily against the chair, propping himself up and trying to steady himself to regain his bearings. However, the effort seemed to exhaust him, and he sank back down, panting and sweating. After a few moments of rest, he mustered up the strength to try again. He did push himself up, but the room seemed to tilt and spin around him. Disheartened, he felt his knees buckle. Desperately, he tried to stay upright, but it was no use. He collapsed back into the chair, gasping for breath and feeling defeated.

Despite his ailing condition, he finally summoned all the courage he had left to slowly stand up and investigate the peculiar surroundings of Katrina Van Tassel's former homestead. With a trembling hand, he reached out to a nearby table for support. When he felt steady enough to walk, he more cautiously and closely inspected the room

and peered into the hallway.  Nothing
seemed out of the ordinary, and no one
seemed to be lurking.  The room's walls
were old and decrepit, and the paint was
peeling off in large flakes that crumbled
under his fingertips.  He took a few
tentative steps towards the hallway,
peering intently into the darkness.  Still,
nothing seemed out of the ordinary there
either.  The place simply looked like an
old, abandoned mansion with a musty
smell that hung heavy in the air and an
eerie silence that made his heartbeat
faster with each passing moment.

   The soft light of dawn seeped
through the window.  It illuminated the
room with a pale yellowish glow, casting
sinister shadows on the walls.  Yes, the
shadows on the walls seemed alive,
animated, contorting, and writhing like
ominous figures.  Their twisting and
turning like menacing figures indeed lent
a creepy and mysterious ambiance to the
space.

   Still quaking from last night's
debilitating experience, he took out his
cell phone to check if anyone texted or

called. His heart sank when he saw that Katherine tried to contact him, and her logged attempts only intensified his dread. Upon reading his cell log, it turned out that both her call and text came at the same time he became frightened to death and fainted in this horrid mansion.

At this point, though, he was too shaken to speculate about the possible connection or explanation. All he could think of was escaping, running from Katrina and her decrepit Van Tassel homestead as fast as possible.

As he turned the doorknob to leave, he felt a sudden and strong gust of wind brush past him. At that moment, a man's barely audible voice embedded within the wind whispered into his ear, "Your pen can be a risky tool to your health. It can even endanger your overall life expectancy."

Feeling the chill in the air now engulfed him while those ominous words were spoken left Graysen's heart racing yet again. Instead of turning around to find the presence lurking in the shadows, he sprinted out the door.

   The cold air hit him like a slap in the face as soon as he stepped out of the house.  Despite the frigid air's numbing sensation, he ran as fast as he could, never daring to look back at Katrina Van Tassel's formerly stately but now haunted and dilapidated residence.

# The Paranormal World

# Is Not Disney World

# (Chapter 13)

As the first rays of sunlight broke, he wearily crawled into his home, his sanctuary.

After a long, unsettling night, he couldn't stop pacing and shaking from his hair-raising spectral entanglement at the old mansion.

Before calling Katherine, he wanted to clear his mind, so he took a long, hot, steamy shower. Seeking to comfort himself, he also hoped to wash away the feeling of dread that lingered. With a clearer mind, he could rationally discuss last night's events with Katherine. He worried she must be distraught about his not texting her when she tried to reach him last night.

Fearing that she must be anxiously awaiting his response, he quickly texted her before jumping into the shower. He wanted her to know he had to skip breakfast but would call her soon to discuss what happened last night in detail.

After luxuriating in a long, steamy, sauna-like shower, he went into the kitchen to fix breakfast and light some fragrant incense that Katherine had given him before they parted last night.

Once he ate and dressed for the day, he felt comfortable opening a conversation with Katherine about last night's ghastly events. After clearing the table of his breakfast dishes, he got his laptop and writing instruments out. In honor of loving his Katherine, he also lit some more of her soothing incense sticks, making a mental note to ask her what he was supposed to expect from this blend. Once he organized himself, he picked up his cell and called Katherine.

"Hello, how are you?" he said with all the tender care and concern that a man in love expresses toward his intended.

"Graysen! Are you alright?" scared Katherine asked. "Yes, I have been worried. The rustling up of the winds on our walk home after dinner still alarms me. When you didn't respond to my call or text, all sorts of thoughts raced through my mind. I paced the floor, wondering if I should go out looking for you or call the police. I don't know why, but I fell asleep on my sofa right after I texted you. I don't know, but it was all so overwhelming last night. So, tell me, are you alright and what happened? Why didn't you respond when I called or texted? I followed up with a text since I thought maybe you shut your ringer off."

Graysen only wanted to reassure her that he was fine but was embarrassed that he wasn't readily available for her call. So, he jumped right into their conversation and said, "You won't believe what happened to me last night. Oh, Katherine! I'm still shaken but ready to talk about it now. Are you sitting down?"

"Yeah, sure, go ahead," the ever-so flustered Katherine said. Graysen started to vividly detail his harrowing experience, "Last night, well, the entire evening was an unforgettable experience, but I stopped at Katrina Van Tassel's abandoned mansion on the way home. I swear, there's an active mystical force there. Believe it or not, I encountered the spirit of Katrina herself and some unidentifiable man. Yes, the spirit of Katrina herself appeared before me. Oh, please! The entire hair-raising encounter sent shivers down my spine and was so intense that I fainted."

Distressed and filled with fear, Katherine sighed into the phone.

Sensing he sounded a bit ridiculous; he didn't want their conversation to be reduced to a dance of skepticism, a clash of the mundane against the magical. So, once again, he asserted, "Really, Katherine! It happened!!! Anyone ever talk about an active mystical force at the mansion?"

Imploring him to remain calm, flustered Katherine said, "Oh, my dear, Graysen, Sleepy Hollow is full of tales and spirits, especially during a full moon, of which there is a Blood Moon on our horizon. But are you sure it wasn't just optical tricks as you wandered in the dark of an old, decaying mansion? Or maybe you just tripped on a loose floorboard?

You know, not everything is a mystical conspiracy..."

Feeling as though he was losing credibility with her, Graysen said, "No, it was a real otherworldly experience, encounter, or whatever you want to label it. The air turned cold, and I heard whispers. Katrina's spirit was there, and the man… was like a shadow, just out of sight. I've never experienced anything like it."

Whatever happened with this conversation, Graysen didn't want to end their conversation with the truth remaining as elusive as the whispers of the past that echoed through the halls of the deserted mansion.

Katherine, loving her Graysen oh so much, sighed and said, "The spirits of the past can be quite convincing, but remember, the mind can also conjure up fears in the dark. Did you give squatters any thought or consideration in what happened to you last night?"

Graysen laughed. "You mean fleeting visitors?" and sighed in relief. He could tell that the woman he loved desired him too. She just wanted to ensure that they examined all possibilities before drawing conclusions about his being drawn into the spirit world by Katrina Van Tassel and some unidentifiable, ruthlessly fiendish man.

Still laughing, Graysen explained his disbelief that he encountered fleeting visitors, "Let me put it this way. Katrina Van Tassel's mansion seems guarded by its own spectral presence, repelling the living who seek to invade its solitude. Based on last night's experience, Katrina herself still watches over her domain, ensuring that her peace remains undisturbed by anyone, including squatters."

Understanding his point, Katherine, too, burst out laughing as he talked. She also cautiously showed in her voice that she was relenting to his argument. Sighing, she said, "Perhaps the mansion is more alive than we thought."

Feeling ever-so connected to Katherine now, Graysen said, "Alive is one way to put it. Katrina Van Tassel declared that she was going to make me hers. Really!!! I kid you not! She truly is a mean one with an evil, nasty aura, too."

Changing her vocal tone to a serious one, Katherine, the witch, said, "Well, if the spirits reached out to you, maybe they sense your connection to the otherworldly? Our relationship, Graysen! Or maybe, just maybe, it was the moon's influence. Either way, take care when wandering into such places."

Despite feeling pleasantly surprised by her statement, old fears stirred within him. He unsuccessfully tried to shake the fears off as he talked. He didn't want to leave the conversation hanging, so he said, "I will. I promise I will, but I can't shake the feeling that there's more to uncover at Katrina's decaying mansion. Interestingly, for instance, your call and text came at the same time that I fainted. So, you really think that the spirit world senses that I have a connection to the spirit world, my beautiful Katherine?"

With mixed emotions, Katherine heard him more fully now. She said, "Oh, Graysen! Exercise caution from now on. Remember what happened after we started to walk home from the restaurant last night? We still don't know what caused it, and I am still spooked by it. Until we get better answers, facing the unknown with someone at your side is always better than challenging a dark world that you don't know anything about. A paranormal world is not a Walt Disney world."

Graysen felt oh so good that he could share his experience with his intended. He also felt her admonishment and wanted to reassure her about their mutual future. So, he happily said, "Thanks, I'll remember that. And, who knows, maybe next time I'll find the proof of a hidden world within Katrina Van Tassel's homestead that will convince even the most skeptical among us."

Sounding dismissive and maybe a bit underwhelmed, Katherine said, "Don't worry about developing proof; Sleepy Hollow will always have its mysteries. The town has a way of watching over itself."

Graysen sighed in relief to be reassuring toward her and then remarked how fascinating Sleepy Hollow was. Curious about another unaddressed point, the reporter in him asked, "Has anyone ever tried to investigate these supernatural claims more scientifically, perhaps during a full moon?"

Thoughtfully, Katherine answered, "Oh, many came with gadgets and gizmos, trying to pierce our town's mystical veil. But Sleepy Hollow's secrets and full moon nights are not to be trifled with. Like the town, the decaying grandeur of Katrina's abandoned mansion holds its mysteries close to its heart."

After Graysen checked the time and his calendar of obligations, he decided he needed to end the conversation here. His laptop's list of upcoming professional deadlines genuinely pressured him to end the conversation. "Okay, well, thank you for sharing your valued insights. Clearly, the legend of the Van Tassel mansion continues to be a captivating chapter in Sleepy Hollow's history."

Katherine, loving Graysen, said, "Indeed, and the stories will continue to flow. Just remember, Mr. Reporter, some truths are best left to the night and the hushed murmurs carried by the wind."

Since his laptop's pressing list distracted his attention, Graysen only partially heard what she said about leaving some things to the whispers carried by the winds. Instead of continuing their conversation, he reassured her that he would still see her for lunch.

When he hung up his phone, he was on Cloud 9. As he emotionally floated about his new residence, he heard more clearly a man's voice repeat the message, "Your pen can be risky to your health. It can even shorten your overall life expectancy." Flabbergasted, he ran to his window but didn't see anyone lurking.

Standing in front of the mirror, he adjusted his tie, combed his hair, and contemplated Katherine's warning that some truths were better left unspoken. These words kept lingering in his mind, making him wonder about the secrets this town might be hiding. However, he was determined to do his job as a newly hired reporter at The Sleepy Hollow Gazette to the best of his abilities. Of course, he also wondered whether the voice he kept hearing was a supernatural force or someone's simple misstep. Would his experience in Sleepy Hollow become another legend whispered in the town's streets? Would it leave all who heard it to wonder and debate, just as he, the reporter, did today?

# The Witching Hour's

# Dark Design

# (Chapter 14)

## A Witch's Incantation

"By the rose's gentle power, I craft this witch's hour! A spell of love, a charm so bright, with my incense burning through it. Beauty's grace and healing's touch, compassion's hand that offers much. I call forth love in Sleepy Hollow's mystic space to this embrace.

With petals soft and scent so sweet, I summon love for two to meet, a witch of old, a scribe of news, their hearts entwined, they'll never lose. This incantation, pure and true, for a love that's ever new. May it guide them, strong and sure, to a bond that will endure.

So may it be, with power cast, this spell of love to hold and last, through rose incense, let it rise, to weave their fates beneath the skies. For a witch and her love so dear, may this charm bring them near. With beauty, love, compassion, healing, their united hearts revealing."

With arms fully extended and a heart filled with a witch's passion,

Katherine took one last grand swirl and found herself face-to-face with Graysen, opening the door to her shop, A Mystical Escape.

"Time for lunch!" he joyfully hollered!

With ear-to-ear smiles, they both fell into an embrace. They continued to hug and kiss as they were so happy to see each other again.

"Graysen, I am so happy to see you again. Are you alright? Did you get stuff done after our talk this morning?" Katherine found it difficult to let go of him as she walked him over to their cozy corner sofa. The same spot where he enjoyed her peanut butter bars.

"Please sit down. Since you have a full day ahead of you, I fixed some sandwiches and tea. Sit, and let me get them."

Graysen eased into the corner sofa, the worn fabric embracing him like an old friend. By now, the room held a comfortable familiarity. Their laughter effortlessly flowing through the air.

Walking over to the lunch tray she

prepared, she started talking about Mediums. "Graysen," she said, "Mediums possess the extraordinary ability to communicate with entities from the spiritual world. Through seances, mediums exercise their exceptional ability to communicate with deceased spirits. They can even facilitate the exchange of messages between the living and the spirit world. So, you and I need to schedule one so that we can move forward with our joint intentions and establish a sense of comfort and closure about what happened to us in the last couple of days. We should never live in fear, Graysen."

Graysen chuckled and spread his arms wide when he said, "Hey, I fainted!"

Katherine appreciated his jovial-like demeanor but wanted him to know she was serious about his safety. Perched on the armrest, her gaze intense, a testament to the battles she fought beyond the mundane world. "Graysen," she began, her voice low, "I need you to understand something. Sleepy Hollow isn't just a quaint town with legends. It's a place where the veil between our world and the supernatural is thin. Dark forces stir, and sometimes they don't take kindly to newcomers as they can threaten our way of life."

With that said, she continued, "Now, about your tumble last night, let's have some calming tea and talk about it. You're not the first to experience the unusual there."

"Like I said, it was more than unusual." a shaken Graysen wailed, "The air turned thick with whispers, and everything, including me, went black! I woke up on the floor!!!"

With a shrug and a sigh of resignation, Katherine responded, "That decaying mansion's history revolves around mystical forces, including ghostly apparitions, mysterious whispers, and unexplained phenomena. It is said that the mansion's walls hold memories and secrets of the past, making it a place of both fascination and fear for Sleepy Hollow's residents."

"Oh, Graysen, with the upcoming full moon, all old stories are resurrected. I just want to rule out whether you tripped on a loose floorboard or (now laughing) you were the victim of squatters or (laughing even more intensely) fleeting visitors, as you call them."

Enjoying her humor, he started to laugh some more himself. At the same time, he said, "I'm a skeptic, Katherine Vanessa Talisman, but even I can't deny the chill that ran down my spine. I think we need to delve deeper into it."

"Okay. Hey, I agree with you." Katherine said. As she touched his arm to extend reassurance, she added, "A séance is what I, your personal Sleepy Hollow enchantress, prescribe." Slightly turning and catching his facial expression, she said, "Oh. Come on. Don't give me that outrageous look!" Showing a sense of wisdom over his lack of commitment, she sternly advised, "We should consult a medium to understand if there's a message or a warning from the spirits for us, a newly minted couple with a connection through me to the otherworld! Graysen, please... I beg you!!! Don't ignore the obvious."

Graysen, rolling his eyes as he got deeper into what Katherine was thinking, said, "A séance? I've never attended one before. Do you think it's necessary?"

Now feeling that adding a sense of fun to their conversation would be wise, Katherine said, "Unless you'd prefer something more… dramatic? I could enlist the aid of a Necromancer! But be warned, they don't bring the dead back in pristine condition. And didn't you say that Katrina wanted to make you hers? And her evil attitude and wicked intentions frightened you?"

Openly laughing at the way Katherine resurrected Katrina's stated desires and ambitions for him, Graysen said, "Okay, okay. You made your point. Let's schedule a séance." Playfully, he added, "I'm not ready for the alternative, Katrina! Yuck!!!"

Relieved that her approach was winning him over to her way of thinking, she summarized their intended plans, "Given the circumstances and expectations set by Katrina, yes, the séance is where we will start. Let's schedule it after the town's Halloween parade. Our schedules should align perfectly for that." Graysen nodded in agreement, appreciating Katherine's strategic thinking and ability to handle the situation with humor. He knew that together, they would navigate the eerie path ahead, ensuring their safety while unraveling the mysteries surrounding Katrina's intentions.

"Oh, Graysen, I want you to feel comfortable working and living here. So, you need to know that the appearance of a full moon on Halloween is a rare event and carries significant cultural and symbolic meaning, especially in the context of Sleepy Hollow, a place steeped in supernatural folklore. As you know, a Blood Moon, the name for a full moon that occurs in October, and a Hunter's Moon hold great significance in many cultures and belief systems. It is believed that during a Blood Moon, the veil between the spirit world and our own is at its thinnest, making it an ideal time for spiritual practices such as seances. On the other hand, The Hunter Moon represents a time of abundance and preparation for the winter months, when hunting and gathering were crucial for survival. Understanding these cultural and symbolic meanings will help you navigate Sleepy Hollow's unique supernatural landscape with greater insight and awareness."

"For a witch from Sleepy Hollow meeting up with her newfound love interest, a Gazette newspaper reporter, on such a night, the Blood Moon could represent a decisive moment of transformation and connection. The Hunter's Moon signifies a time of focusing on preparations for the coming winter, which could metaphorically translate to the witch and her love interest preparing for a new chapter in their lives."

"The fact that this meeting would occur on Halloween, during an hour when the veil between the living and the dead is said to be thinnest, could add an additional layer of mystery and magic to the encounter. The witch and the reporter—Yes! Us, Graysen--may find themselves caught between the realms of the supernatural and reality. Deepening the bond as they navigate this enchanted evening together would add an extra layer of significance, suggesting a deep and mystical connection. Graysen, the rare occurrence of a full moon on Halloween, which only happens every 18 or 19 years, could imply that our meeting is a once-in-a-lifetime event filled with potential and magic.

"Yes, Graysen, think! An alignment of celestial events like a full moon on Halloween could symbolize a convergence of cosmic forces, indicating that our meeting holds a profound destiny or purpose. It's as if the universe has conspired to bring us together on this extraordinary night, where anything is possible and the boundaries between reality and fantasy blur.  Events in our newfound relationship often herald significant developments. A full moon on Halloween is the perfect catalyst for something extraordinary. It's like the universe conspires to unite and guide us on a remarkable journey. A heightened sense of destiny or fate comes into play."

As Katherine pirouetted to emphasize her statements, Graysen chuckled and laughed. But when her shop's door simultaneously blew open with a gale force, stunned Graysen looked to Katherine for an explanation. She simply shrugged and said, "It's windy outside. I have to do something about replacing that old door's locks."

Shaking his head and laughing about how their conversation shaped up, he swallowed, the weight of their situation settling on his shoulders. He finally said, "Alright, I trust your judgment, my beautiful Sleepy Hollow sorceress. Let's do it! After all, what's Halloween in this town without a little supernatural adventure as the Blood Moon fills the night sky?"

Katherine's enthusiasm overflowed as she realized she touched Graysen's inner wisdom without arguing about hocus-pocus. She knew their shared love for the mystical and the unknown would make their Halloween night unforgettable. As they prepared to face whatever supernatural encounters awaited them, Katherine couldn't help but feel a sense of excitement and anticipation for the magical journey they were about to embark on together. She took another whirl and exclaimed, "Exactly!" and suddenly changed her tone. She now sounded like an ominous witch by eerily stating, "And don't worry, we'll figure this out together. Now, drink your tea; trust me, it'll calm your nerves."

As he obediently drank his tea, he thanked her for her thoughtfulness. The fragrant brew curled around him, chasing away the chill that clung to the edges of his nerves. "You always know how to make things better."

She then changed her tone yet again and said, "Turning to a much more fun subject, what are you wearing in our town's Halloween parade this year?

Chuckling, he said, "Well, I was thinking of being a reporter, yeah, you know, I'll wear my usual suit and tie; maybe I'll get one of those typed REPORTER identification cards that men used to tuck into the front of their hat's bands and wear one of those fake over-sized eyeglasses with nose and mustache attached. Wouldn't that be a great way to greet the crowd?"

As their conversation about how he should present himself in the parade progressed, so did their rockin' and rollin' with laughter on the sofa.

"But seriously," Katherine said, "you should think of something more creative. Something that matches your personality and style."

Taking a break from their laughing, Graysen asked, "Like what?"

Caught up in this uproarious humorous exchange about Halloween costumes, Katherine suggested that he dress as a Necromancer, complete with a flowing black robe and a staff adorned with wizardry symbols. Graysen's eyes lit up at the idea, imagining himself casting spells and enchanting the crowd with his mystical presence. It was a perfect fit for his love of all things darkly supernatural, and he couldn't wait to bring his unique character to life in the parade.

In keeping with the spirit, Graysen

jovially asked, "Well, just how does necromancy work? Tell me, tell me now, my Katherine! Fill my mind, heart, and most importantly, soul with how necromancy works!!!"

Without warning, Katherine changed her tone and mannerisms into a spine-chilling woman. Her voice dropped to a low, haunting whisper as she began to explain the dark arts of necromancy, detailing the rituals and incantations used to communicate with the dead. Graysen listened intently, his eyes wide with fascination and a hint of trepidation. As Katherine delved deeper into the subject, he couldn't help but feel a strange mixture of excitement and unease. The secrets she revealed seemed to awaken something within him, igniting a newfound curiosity that he couldn't ignore.

He felt slightly unnerved by the power necromancy held over life and death. The more he learned, the more he realized that bringing his unique character to life in the parade would require a deeper understanding of the dark arts than he had initially anticipated. Realizing that this Halloween costume idea might be more than just a playful suggestion, the thought of embodying such a captivating character in the parade ignited a newfound excitement within him, fueling his determination to master the intricacies of necromancy and make his costume genuinely unforgettable. With that, she says, "A very dark and dangerous form of magic, Necromancy involves communicating with the dead by summoning their spirits as apparitions or visions for the purpose of divination, imparting the means to foretell future events and discover hidden knowledge. It is said that necromancy requires immense skill and concentration, as one must navigate the delicate balance between the living and the deceased realms. The allure of this forbidden art further enticed him as he yearned to unlock the secrets of the afterlife and unravel the mysteries that lay beyond our mortal existence. Sometimes categorized under death magic, the term is occasionally also used in a more general sense to refer to black magic or witchcraft as a whole."

Graysen, acting like he is getting the weird and dangerous vibe that Katherine filled their conversation with, said, "Wow!!! It does sound scary. What else do you want me to know about Necromancers?

Katherine paused for a moment, her eyes filled with a mix of caution and fascination. "Well, Graysen, it's important to understand that not all necromancers are inherently evil or malicious. While some may use their powers for dark purposes, others strive to maintain the balance between life and death, using their abilities to heal and communicate with spirits. It's a complex and misunderstood practice that requires great responsibility and respect for the natural order of things."

A bit confused, Graysen asked, "Are they also witches?"

Katherine continued talking as though she was in some entrenched altered state. "No, not all necromancers are witches," Katherine replied, her voice steady yet filled with a hint of excitement. "Witches typically focus on harnessing elemental magic and casting spells, while necromancers specifically delve into the realm of death and spirits. Although there may be some overlap in their knowledge and abilities, they are distinct practices with unique skills and rituals. A Necromancer is a person who uses witchcraft or sorcery to reanimate dead people or to foretell the future. Necromancers possess the ability to communicate with spirits and manipulate the energy of the deceased, often seeking their guidance or assistance. This connection to the realm of death sets them apart from witches, who primarily work with elemental forces and nature."

"Additionally, necromancers may possess divination skills, allowing them to glimpse into the future or gain insights from beyond the mortal plane. While they are not necessarily witches, they often use similar methods and tools. The most important thing to know about them is that their power usually corrupts them. They have no respect for the natural order of life and death."

Graysen, picking up on the point

that a Necromancer is commonly corrupt, took on a more serious tone when he asked, "How do they reanimate dead people? Is it through some sort of dark magic or manipulation of the life force? Can they control the reanimated beings, or are they merely puppets under their command? Like,...do they make zombies or something?"

"No, not exactly." Katherine said, "Zombies are mindless creatures controlled by the Necromancer's will. They are usually created by infusing a corpse with a dark energy that animates it. Necromancers can also create skeletons, ghouls, and other undead beings by using bones, flesh, and blood as their materials."

Horrified, Greysen stuttered and asked, "How...how can they do that?"

Katherine explained, "They use a mixture of rituals, spells, and incantations that draw upon the power of the underworld, the realm of the dead souls. They also use objects that are associated with death, such as skulls, coffins, graveyards, and corpses. They often perform their magic at night, under the moon's light, or during special occasions like Halloween, Blood Moon, or the winter solstice."

"And why do they do that?" Graysen asked, "I don't understand. What do they specifically gain from it?"

Katherine continued to explain, "Necromancers have different motives and goals. Some of them are driven by curiosity, greed, or revenge. They want to know the secrets of the afterlife, to acquire wealth and power, or to harm their enemies. Some of them are obsessed with immortality and seek to cheat death by transferring their souls into undead bodies. Some of them are simply evil and enjoy causing pain and suffering to the living and the dead."

"That's awful!" Graysen gasped like he had just drank poison. "How can they be stopped?"

Katherine shrugged, "Necromancers are hard to stop because they can access many resources and allies. They often have followers, servants, or minions that do their bidding. They also have allies among the world's dark forces, such as demons, vampires, and werewolves. They are very cunning and secretive and hide their activities from the public."

Looking at Greyson, whose mouth gaped wide open, Katherine continued, "Witches can fight them with our own magic. We can use spells and charms that protect us from attacks and weaken or banish their undead creations. We can also use our divination skills to discover their plans and locations and expose their secrets. We can also ally ourselves with other forces of good, such as angels, fairies, and dragons.

Graysen's face filled with admiration, "You're amazing, my most beautiful Katherine, my most bewitching enchantress. I'm so glad we met. I feel like I am floating on a cloud when I am with you!!!"

Blushing, Katherine's softness radiated from within. She acknowledged his compliment with a simple "Thank you. I'm glad we met, too!"

Filled with the look of love, Graysen asked, "May I ask you

something else?"

"Sure!" Katherine slipped back into a giggling mode and back onto the sofa they were sitting on. "Yeah, sure, but will it involve my waving a wand and saying mystical words? Or conjuring up a connection to the world's natural forces and using them to shape reality according to your will?"

He moved in to hug her as he asked, "May I kiss you?"

With an ear-to-ear smile, Katherine let the forces do the rest.

As her shop's door chime rang, Katherine, now giddy and weak at the knees, waved goodbye to Graysen. She blew him one final kiss and, with a wave of her hand, said, "I'll see you for dinner. Between now and then, don't let the ghouls and goblins of Sleepy Hollow drag you into their underworld."

Graysen, too, laughed and stumbled out of her shop, A Mystical Escape, as he replayed various parts of their hilarious conversation in his mind and kept nodding in agreement with her expectation that they, once again, would meet for dinner.

As he rounded the street corner, though, he just about toppled. He seemed to have lost his footing as he simultaneously heard that now familiar, deep, sinister laugh. He looked around for the cause of his near fall and where the menace might be positioned. Frustrated by not seeing anything or anyone, he shook his head and mumbled, "Sleepy Hollow invests too much in their Halloween rituals." To which he heard the same man's deep and forbidding voice laughingly say, "Yeah, sure..."

# The Witching Hour

# (Chapter 15)

Curious, Katherine stepped to one side to see who entered her Mystical Escape shop when the store's door chimed. To her delight, Graysen stepped into her shop and excitedly started talking about the town's decorations for the Halloween Parade. To him, a breathtaking display of nature's beauty filled the town's parade route. The intricately carved pumpkins and vibrant colors of the other customary Halloween decorations filled the streets while an exquisite scent of fall flowers filled the air. The mild winds caused the leaves to rustle just enough to create a natural symphony of music. "What a night it is going to be! It's just gorgeous out there, Katherine! The town's organizers did a stunning job!!! The street vendors are all lined up, too. I can't wait to see everyone in their costumes parading around town and milling about and for us to be a part of it!"

Grinning like a Cheshire cat, she called him to come to where she stood. With her arm fully extended and holding an intriguing concoction that looked like a witches' brew, she said, "I've got a joke for you!"

Graysen, happy to be in her shop as the air always crackled with magic, called out, "Okay!" as he walked over to where she was standing.

Katherine, with her eyes sparkling like ancient spells, grinned and said, "Knock, knock!" Graysen, intrigued, played along. "Who's there?" he responded with a light laugh.

"Boo," Katherine whispered, her voice carrying secrets from centuries past. Graysen leaned in, intrigued. "Boo, who?" he replied, lips puckering in anticipation.

In the dim candlelight of Katherine's A Mystical Escape boutique, her laughter flowed through the air as though it mirrored the ancient winds flowing through the town's haunted woods. Pulling him closer, she teased, "BooHoo? Don't cry!" With her lips brushing against his, she then finished her knock-knock joke. "There's no need for tears tonight. It's party time. It's Halloween!" And in that enchanted moment, as the full Blood Moon peeked through the town's twisted branches, they kissed—not as a witch and a reporter—but as two people lost in the magic of love.

Taking a step back and releasing her from his hold, he asked, "What are you holding there?"

She beamed when she said, "Are you ready to have some fun?"
After he nodded yes, she continued her greeting by saying, "Welcome to a Sleepy Hollow Halloween celebration. All of us locals enjoy this customary Halloween drink. It is a beloved tradition among us locals!"

Holding it out for his inspection, she said, "This simple mix of vodka, soft drink mix, soda, and sherbet makes it look like a bubbling cauldron of magic. If you add some dry ice for an extra effect, be careful not to touch or drink it!!! PLEASE! The dry ice is just for appearances. No passing out allowed!"

Taking the drink from her and making his way to their corner sofa, he asked, "So, you mentioned on the phone this afternoon that you want me to watch out for any unusual occurrences tonight. Hmm? Can you explain yourself a bit more now, my mysterious companion?"

"Well, here's the inside scoop, Mr. Reporter," Katherine said, "after you left, I gave the issue some thought and decided that you should dress as the Headless Horseman for the parade. After the parade, we will attend our séance in the cemetery during the witching hour. With the full Blood Moon casting a crimson glow, the sky will provide ample light to fully immerse ourselves in the otherworldly séance." Shrugging, he ended the conversation with a simple "Okay."

Shifting in his seat, he changed his tone to a more serious one and said, "Something incredibly bizarre happened to me when I left you after lunch. I heard the same man's sinister laugh again as I turned the corner. Creepy!!! Is there someone in town who adopts this persona and assumes the responsibility of stirring the cauldron?" With that comment, Graysen scrutinized his drink a bit more and wondered if Katherine knew of a local legend or tradition associated with the mysterious laughter. Perhaps a secret society in town, like the Beekman Circle, embraced the occult and performed peculiar rituals during special events like the Blood Moon.

Katherine continued to prepare their light pre-Halloween parade dinner while he revealed his encounter with the unidentifiable man. She turned sideways toward him when he detailed his ghastly post-lunch encounter. Katherine considered the possibilities but just drew a blank. Kind of laughing, she said, "You've got me at a total loss. No, no, I never heard of anyone or group devoting themselves to frightening others. After all, it doesn't seem rather neighborly."

Amused, Graysen laughed, too, at the thought that someone forgot that Sleepy Hollow was a kind and gentle town. The menacing fool definitely was overstepping the town's established image, Sleepy Hollow's gentile reputation!

Shaking his head, drinking his holiday drink, he breathed a deep sigh that conveyed a sense of resignation. "Oh, well..."

As Katherine approached their corner, she put their dinner tray down. Sliding in next to him on the cozy sofa, she kissed him on the cheek and reassuredly said, "Happy Halloween! I am so happy that you moved here and will enjoy the rest of your days living and working among us. I personally am so happy to embrace you!"

She placed his dinner plate in front of him and suggested that he serve himself. She planned a quick dinner for them since he needed to go home to change into his costume and come back for her. Then, they would join the spirited energy of the townspeople for the parade and festivities.

As he served himself, he said, "You know what else happened this afternoon?" Reaching to fill her own plate, she turned to him and shook her head no.

"Well, about 3 p.m., I looked out my window and noticed the fog lifting. Within the fog, a shocking vision caught my eye. I could swear that I saw your image. It was like in a cloud formation."

Now, thinking the sweetest and most loving thoughts about him, Katherine blushed and said, "Really, Graysen?"

He nodded yes and said, "Yes, I am not kidding. The billowing clouds within the mist formed a distinctive image, leaving me to wonder if it was a message from the celestial forces."

Katherine's eyes grew wide as she exclaimed, "WOW! We really need to take a minute to review the possibilities. For instance, a lifting fog could signify a new chapter in our lives, changes entering our lives, or we are ready to embrace a new adventure. On the downside," she said, shaking her head with a deep sense of dismay, "the lifting fog could mean our romance will end or be gravely interrupted."

Graysen, looking horrified, allowed Katherine to continue. "A more daring interpretation revolves around the revelation of a mystery, unveiling secrets, or even discovering something hidden. Suppose the sign is centered on you, Graysen. In that case, it could be forewarning that you will stumble upon some unexpected news or story. A loss of dreams or imagination can be at the root of the message."

Graysen's ashen face just looked like the idea of having fun tonight abruptly died, like a sudden death. Katherine reached out to comfort him and said, "I am sorry, but don't put too much meaning into it. It can mean we are ready to embrace a new adventure and nothing more than that!"

Putting on a happier face, Katherine encouragingly smiled and exclaimed, "A toast, Graysen! A toast." Graysen immediately lifted his glass as she delivered their first of many Halloween celebration toasts:

"I love it that you are joining me on this Halloween night.
You have witnessed the wonders and horrors of Sleepy Hollow, the land of legends and lore.
You have seen the Old Dutch church, the haunted bridge, the twisted trees, and the ancient graves.
You have heard the howls of the wolves, the witches' cackles, the ghosts' screams, and the whispers of the wind.
You have felt the chill of the air, the touch of the moon, the power of the spells, and the warmth of my heart, Graysen!
You are a brave, curious soul seeking truth and mystery.
You are a reporter, a storyteller, a writer of history and fantasy.
You are a partner, a companion of passion and romance.
You are the one I want, the one I need, the one I choose.
So, let us toast our shared adventure, magic, mystery, and love this Halloween.
Here's to you, Graysen!"

"Now, down the hatch with your Sleepy Hollow Halloween special!"

"Wow! Katherine, that was great, absolutely amazing!!! The holiday drink, dinner, and now this heartfelt toast, what incredible things are next on our list for this evening's festivities?"

Well, you have to go home, change into your spectral Headless Horseman costume, and come back here. Afterward, we will join the others for our Sleepy Hollow parade and high-spirited town merrymaking, complete with dancing in the streets. Our grand finale for this Halloween will be under the cloak of the 3 a.m. witching hour. We will enter the cemetery's hallowed grounds to begin our séance dressed in full costume!"

"Okay, okay." zealous Graysen reassuringly said, "and, hey, my beautiful enchantress, I'm so excited about tonight's Halloween parade and party. It's going to be a blast! I personally cannot wait to see what "The Legend of Sleepy Hollow" pranksters pull."

Katherine's spirits soared as his infectious enthusiasm invigorated her.

She felt rejuvenated! Giggling through their playful banter, she reminded him that Halloween was the best time for her to be a witch!!! With a mischievous glint in her eye, she impishly waved her hands around as if casting a spell and chuckled at the thought of all the magical possibilities that lay ahead.

Gearing up for the soon-to-start street festival, Graysen couldn't help but praise Katherine's talents." Yeah, you always have the most amazing costumes and spells. Speaking of which, what are you going to wear tonight?"

Katherine said, "Well, as I said, after lunch, I thought that something fun and spooky-like would be us going as a necromancy couple, people who can raise the dead. To me, you being the Headless Horseman and me, your Bride, sounded the best. So, I took the liberty of getting you a black cloak with a pumpkin mask and arranged delivery to your home. I will wear a gothic-style wedding dress with a matching veil. I also ordered a lantern to carry. We should be the happy couple of tonight's festivities."

Seeing that Graysen enjoyed her dramatic costume selection, especially since it also will be their coming out as Sleepy Hollow's new couple, she beamed and said, "The costumes are scary, but we will have an incredibly spectacular time parading around town in them."

Wide-eyed, Graysen nodded in agreement and said, "Yeah! That's pretty cool. I think we'll make an out-of-this-world Mr. & Mrs.!"

Confident that she had made all the right decisions for the evening, Katherine assuredly gushed, "Me too. I can't wait to see you in your Headless Horseman costume. You'll look so dashing, so otherworldly as my spouse!"

As he leaned into her, he wrapped his arm around her and whispered, "And you'll look so gorgeous, so splendid as My Bride, Katherine! You'll be the most bewitching witch in Sleepy Hollow and the most enchanting woman I know!"

She couldn't hold back her happiness anymore; she gushed, "Aww, thank you. You're so sweet. I love you!"

Looking deep into her eyes,

Graysen confessed and declared, "I love you too, Katherine! Happy Halloween, my love."

They basked in the magic of their deep connection. Rapture, bliss, Seventh Heaven, and Cloud 9 feelings filled their shared aura. Given the magnitude of their intense feelings for each other, a compelling need to fill this moment with memorable things became essential and urgent.

Katherine said, "Tonight is a Blood Moon! That means it's a very powerful night for magic. And you know how there's a cemetery near the party venue? That means it's a very spooky place for adventure. And you know how I'm a witch, and you're a necromancer for this evening? That means we have a unique connection and special bond with the dead."

Laughing, Graysen said, "Okay, now tell me, where you are going with this conversation? You want to do the séance tonight, don't you?"

Curling up in his arms and nestling, Katherine said, "Yes, I do. I think contacting the spirits of Sleepy Hollow would be so much fun and romantic. Maybe we could even talk to the Headless Horseman himself. What do you say?"

Graysen, thinking Katherine's thoughts through, said, "Well, I'm not going to lie. It sounds a bit scary. But it's also kind of exciting. And I trust you. You're the expert on these things. So, sure, why not? Let's try to talk to the man, the Headless Horseman, himself!"

Katherine openly showed her happiness and excitedly said, "I'm so happy you're on board. Our séance will be mind-blowing. Of course, we do have to wait for the right time."

Taken aback, Graysen quizzically asked, "The witching hour?"

"Yes, the witching hour," Katherine lovingly said, "the hour between 3 and 4 a.m. when the veil between the worlds is the thinnest. That's when the spirits are most active and responsive. It's also the most dangerous time, so we must be careful."

Looking at his alluring bride-for-the-evening and his wanna-be bride-to-be with a sense of resignation, he said, "Okay, I see. So, we'll enjoy the parade and orchestrated fun with all the townspeople. Afterward, we'll come back here for a bit and then sneak out to the cemetery for a 3 a.m. séance, all the while dressed as the Headless Horseman and his Bride? And my costume is presently waiting at my house?"

Katherine hugged him to reassure him, "Exactly! That's the plan!!! Don't fret! I'll bring everything we need. Candles, salt, chalk, a Ouija board, a pendulum, and some protection charms. We'll be safe and sound."

"Okay, sounds good!" Graysen exclaimed, "I'm looking forward to us spending the entire evening together as you are so determined. But I have to ask, what should I expect to happen during the seance? Since I've never done anything like this, can you tell me how it works?"

"Well, it's not that complicated." Katherine said, "It's actually quite simple. We'll find a serene spot in the cemetery, preferably near a grave or a tombstone.

Then, we'll draw a circle with chalk and salt around us to create a sacred space. We light the area with softly flickering candles to set the mood and place them around the circle. This also helps to create a warm and inviting atmosphere. As we settle in, we'll sit down and hold hands to create a bond of love and trust. Forging a connection built on love and trust, we'll use the tools to communicate with the spirit world, the Ouija board, or the pendulum. We'll ask them questions, and they'll answer us by moving the pointer on the Ouija board or the pendulum. We'll be respectful and polite and thank them for their time. And we'll be careful not to break the circle or to invite any unwanted entities. We end the seance by saying goodbye and closing the circle. And that's it. That's how we do a seance."

"That's pretty sensational!" Straightening up and looking at Katherine, a little awe-struck, he said, "I am amazed and a little dazed to think that we're going to talk to the dead during the dead of the night. Will they be friendly, or will they have anything interesting to say? How about fascinating insights or intriguing revelations?

Katherine said, "Well, I can't guarantee anything. The spirits are unpredictable and mysterious. Sometimes, they're helpful and friendly; at other times, they're mischievous and prankish; occasionally, they're angry and vengeful. It depends on who they are, how they died, and what they want. Overall, though, I think we'll be fine. We're not here to harm or disturb them. We're here to learn and connect with them. And maybe have some fun. Who knows, maybe they'll be curious about us too. Maybe they'll have some questions for us. Maybe they'll even like us."

"Yeah, maybe." Graysen tried to take in all Katherine's information and assess his feelings. "That would be cool." he said, "I wonder what they'll think of our costumes. You know, will they be amused or offended? Do you think they'll recognize us as the Headless Horseman and you, my enchantress, as my Headless Horseman Bride?"

"I don't know." Katherine said,

shaking her head, "Maybe. Maybe not. Perhaps they'll think we're impostors. Possibly, they'll think we're admirers. For all I know, they'll think we're hilarious or insulting. It may be that they'll think we're cute, awesome, or crazy. Their impression could even be that we are something they've never previously seen, like deranged! It can be chaotic!!!"

"I am impressed! Katherine, you're really good at this." Graysen said as he sat up straighter, showing a heightened sense of attention. "You have so many possible avenues. I guess we'll have to wait and see which one materializes. Either way, I'm sure it'll be hauntingly unforgettable. I'm thrilled that we're doing this together. You're the best partner I could ever ask for. I love you so much."

"I love you too, Graysen! You're the best! Let's make this a night to remember for us as a couple. I, Kathrine Vanessa Talisman, do not intend to share you with Katrina Van Tassel!"

"'Til death do us part, Katherine?" Graysen asked with an ear-to-ear smile, and Katherine responded as Graysen hoped,'"Til death do us part!"

Graysen jolted, "What just shattered?"

"I don't know," said Katherine, trembling and frightened by the explosion. Composing herself, she said, "Probably some party-goer dropping something. Pumpkins are often dropped with people decorating or tripping over decorations this time of year. We'll check later. Right now, we have to get ready for the town's parade! You need to go home, change, come back, and then we'll join the others in the streets. Let's go, go, go...before the sounds of the drums start in the street!!!"

With the Blood Moon rising over the trees, Graysen exited A Mystical Escape to go home and change into his Headless Horseman Halloween costume.

# An Old Flame

# (Chapter 16)

In the haunted town of Sleepy Hollow, New York, Graysen, a newly hired young and curious journalist from the Sleepy Hollow Gazette, has been digging for secrets and unearthing hidden truths many think should remain buried. As he unwittingly stirs up the fury of restless spirits and awakens the wrath of vengeful phantoms, he becomes obsessed with his investigation, spending more and more time investigating rumors. Some of the stories that fuel and capture his ever-growing curiosity are reports of screams and howls heard in dark woods during the wee hours of the morning, more specifically around 3 a.m.... the witching hour. The screams locals heard now show themselves as echoes of a sinister warning of impending doom. As the gossip builds, tension and the chilling backdrop to his unfolding investigation mounts. The clues, the horror, and the mystery continue to escalate.

When Graysen stepped out of Katherine's Mystical Escape shop, the sight of the full Blood Moon sitting majestically in the sky filled him with an overwhelming sense of trepidation, as if the bloody orb was a sign of something ominous to come this evening. A feeling of unease washed over him, and he wondered, "As the clock strikes three, will Katherine and I unleash dark forces upon the world with our witching hour seance? Will the troubled spirits of the dead rise and bring about the end of our days? Is this possibly the night we summon the apocalypse with our unholy ritual? Oh Katherine, please!!! Will we witness the final judgment of mankind as we contact the other side? Is this Blood Moon an omen about what our upcoming attempt to communicate with the restless souls of Sleepy Hollow will yield?"

Between the sight of the full Blood Moon sitting in the air like a nightmarish beacon for the evening's activities and the grave concerns it stirred within him, Graysen was compelled to catch his breath as he trudged homeward, his footsteps muffled by fallen leaves. The chilling sensation filling the evening air also caused Graysen to shudder and gasp! The air clung to him like a shroud, and the hairs on his neck's nape stood at attention. His breath materialized in the frigid air, each exhale a ghostly wisp. As the temperature plummeted, Graysen's heart raced from exertion. The branches quivered, and the bark felt like frozen flesh. Oh, in pain he recoiled. Was this sudden drop in temperature, deathly cold, a display of some historic pact with the devil! He felt the weight of destiny settling upon him. He prayed to the forgotten gods.

As the Blood Moon watched over him, Graysen continued to shiver uncontrollably but comforted himself with warming and uplifting thoughts. He prayed that his girlfriend's magical powers could somehow conjure up warmer temperatures as the outdoor air became unbearable. He considered running home to keep warm and made a mental note to wear long johns under his Headless Horseman costume.

Despite the cold numbing his fingers, he decided to switch his mindset to a sense of enchantment, excitement, and anticipation. He knew that he and Katherine would be the talk of the town, and they might even make front-page coverage in the local Gazette. As a newly minted Sleepy Hollow couple, he couldn't help but feel a sense of pride and joy that he would marry the town's witch in the Old Dutch Church within a year.

With a smile and a quickened pace, he noticed the church in the offing. He felt his heart beat faster as he saw it looming ahead. The sight filled him with utter joy and anticipation as he imagined the day that he and Katherine would stand at the altar to exchange their marital vows, ready to embark on a lifetime of togetherness. With every step he took closer to the church, the more he loved her, even if she was a witch who dabbled in otherworldly things, like the paranormal. He happily looked forward to crossing the threshold into a realm beyond reason with her by his side. No sooner had he finished that thought than his breath misted. He tasted copper—the flavor of fear.

Seeing the Old Dutch Church close at hand turned his sprint into a dance on air, feeling light as a feather, as if he was weightless. He laughed, "Oh, my captivating enchantress, my bewitching beauty, my alluring bride, I just have this nagging fear that you will awaken something that has been sleeping for ages with our 3 a.m. séance. Probably some ancient warlock, a black magician, or worse, a master of evil! Ha! Oh, what am I letting her get me into? Tonight, will the fragile veil tear during our 3 a.m. seance? She probably will end up hooking me up with Katrina yet!!!"

With the most magnificent and superb visions of his upcoming nuptials etched into his mind, he hastily decided to detour and quickly stop at this beautiful and antiquated house of worship. Since he was here, he couldn't resist the urge to step inside and refresh his memory of the architecture's grandeur and the solemn atmosphere. The intricate details of the church's design, from the stained-glass windows to the high arching ceilings, never failed to impress him. The peaceful ambiance of the church was a welcome respite from the hustle and bustle of the outside world, and he took a moment to breathe in the quiet tranquility before continuing on his way.

Upon reaching the church's front door, he noticed it was open and inviting visitors inside. His heart raced excitedly as he entered the building's dimly lit and musty interior. What he did not know then was that the church's long-held secrets buried deep within it would soon unravel and forever change the course of his life.

As he innocently gazed around, every detail seemed to come alive in his mind. From the carvings on the wooden pews to the mesmerizing stained-glass windows that filtered the sunlight into a kaleidoscope of colors, he eyed the entire area with awe and disbelief. He actually was going to be married here!

It was a moment of quiet contemplation as he mentally and emotionally readied himself for the soon-to-be life-changing event, the legal minting of Mr. & Mrs.!

His eyes started to study the pulpit. Yes, the pulpit where Ichabod preached and where the priest will now stand for his and Katherine's wedding. Beyond it, a sign hung on a small door. It disappointingly read, "Do Not Enter!" No, trespassing, eh?

As Graysen grappled with this sudden disappointment, he also felt a surge of curiosity, which consumed him. He wondered, why entering beyond the small door was forbidden and what was behind that door? What secrets did this mysterious door conceal?

At first, he could feel his steps toward the door falter.  Was it a premonition, a harbinger of his own demise? His internal compass wavered, torn between journalistic zeal and an inexplicable dread that clung to the church's very timbers.

After he looked around, he realized that no one else was in the church. With no official to stop him or explain this door's posted sign, his sense of adventure took over! He decided to take a peek and pressed onward. He assuredly walked towards the door. His hand trembled, though, as he slightly pushed the door open. The path narrowed and led to an equally narrow staircase. Down the stairs sat the church basement.

He could faintly hear dripping water and wondered if it was safe to venture down those stairs to find out why the water dripped. As he wrestled with his thoughts, he felt a heightened sense of alertness and fear, making his skin crawl.

Ultimately, his curiosity compelled him to take a cautious step forward and officially step inside. He closed the door behind him to keep his search quiet. Unaware of the grave consequences ahead, he held onto the railing as he quietly and carefully descended the creaking stairs. His first thought was that this could not be a space routinely frequented. The smell of the air was musty instead of well-ventilated. There also was a build-up of dampness in the air, which probably added to the chill. As he concentrated on his descent, Katherine's warning about loose floorboards came back to him. Chuckling to himself about loose floorboards, squatters, fleeting visitors, and all other strange spectral forms of existence like Katrina Van Tassel and friends, he tried even harder to focus more on safely descending these squeaking stairs.

A faintly lit room with stone walls and floor awaited him when he reached the bottom of the stairwell. The creepy quarters held shelves along the walls, and those shelves were filled with old books and dusty jars. Cluttered papers with scribbling on them and scattered tools lay across an aged, cracked, and weathered wooden table.

Graysen apprehensibly walked over to the table. Picking up one of the papers to examine it, he discovered a map of Sleepy Hollow enhanced with some fascinating markings. He recognized several landmarks: the church, the bridge, the cemetery, and, of course, Katrina Van Tassel's old decaying mansion!

But several symbols he didn't understand: a skull, a cross, a star, and a horseshoe. Were they demonic symbols hidden away in the basement?

Graysen felt excitement and inquisitiveness as he took out his notebook and cell. Eager to capture these images, he wanted both sketches and photographs of the symbols. He wondered what they meant. Were they cryptic symbols? They could have been divinatory messages. Was there any connection to the Headless Horseman, or were they just harmless decorations?

With every passing minute, though, Graysen's bad luck intensified. His incurable inquisitiveness led him down a treacherous path, a path of no return. In his quest to learn more, he unknowingly made a fatal mistake that sealed his fate. Touching and tampering with sacred symbols triggered grave repercussions from the spiritual world, Katrina's world.

As he wondered what these possibly demonic symbols hidden away in a basement meant and, more importantly, who drew them, he heard a loud, deafening rumble and then a blood-curdling scream. The wall shook, leaving him feeling unnerved. When the symbols started to glow with a thick blood-red hue, sheer terror coursed through his veins. So paralyzed with fright, he dropped his flashlight and cell. Recoiling in fear, he stumbled backward. As he sort of fell back and crouched down, wincing, a ghastly, chilling, and terrifying vision flashed before his eyes.

Oh My God! What is next?" he shrieked. Just when the world seemingly came to a halt, the weird, unexplainable happenings came to a standstill. Suddenly, there was no more evidence of a supernatural presence in the room.

Pausing to gain control of his mind and emotions, he focused on his breathing. Then, he expanded his concentration to all the other aspects of the room. Feeling confident that no spiritual force flooded the room's aura, he felt as though he steadied himself sufficiently enough to study the four symbols of a skull, cross, star, and horseshoe!

Pulling from his recall and testing his memory, he tried to recollect details about how a skull can represent death, mortality, piracy, poison, or danger. The cross can also symbolize faith, hope, or salvation. In some contexts, it may be a protective or healing symbol against evil forces like the Headless Horseman! A star's geometric shape can have various meanings depending on the number of points, orientation, and color. It may represent celestial bodies like the sun, moon, and planets or concepts like light, wisdom, or spirituality. In some traditions, it may symbolize magic, occultism, or astrology. While a horseshoe attached to horses' hooves protects them from wear and tear, it is also recognized as a symbol of luck and protection, especially when hung upside down over a door or a wall. It is believed to ward off evil spirits and attract good fortune. The shape of the horseshoe may also resemble a crescent moon, a symbol of fertility and femininity.

As he worked to recall more information, he frantically rummaged around the room to find where his cell fell. If he could only get to his phone and do a Google search. He could more rapidly get more crucial details and more significant information.

While he scoured the place for his missing mobile phone, he also mused about who the mysterious artist behind the creation of these peculiar and seemingly cryptic symbols was.

He turned his attention to the other papers strewn across the table and started to read through them. Astounded, he found notes hastily written in old, vintage-styled handwriting. They were about the legend of the Headless

Horseman but with some strange pivotal twists. Unsettling and peculiar deviations. Unfamiliar turns that Graysen had never heard.

Feeling overwhelmed by all this startling and challenging information, astounded, Graysen struggled to regain and maintain his composure. He then staggered over to the table to actually read these papers. They made claims that:

- The Headless Horseman is not a ghost, but a devilishly elusive creature summoned by an ancient cult. He is extremely difficult to catch or find, given his often mischievous or deceptive nature woven from moonlight and vengeance. He effortlessly slips through the veil between both worlds.

- The cult used to perform dark rituals and sacrifices in the depths of the church basement every Halloween. Records show people, town's people disappeared, vanished without a trace. (Trembling, he dumbfoundedly wondered if this barbaric ritual was something that his sweet Katherine Vanessa Talisman, his most beautiful enchantress, orchestrated for their seance. Oh My God!!! The spirit world will empower Katrina Van Tassel with the upper hand yet! And the thought that otherworldly figures could hold supernatural strength governing his life sent goosebumps throughout his entire body!)

- Ichabod Crane, a mysterious cult member, stole The Horseman's head. (Ichabod! Did Ichabod Crane have any affiliations with a secret society? Which secret societies were present in Sleepy Hollow during his time? The Beekman Circle?)

- Leaving a trail of death in his wake, the Horseman relentlessly continues his endless search for his severed head. He will kill anyone who gets in his way!!! No one is safe from his wrath; he will stop at nothing to eliminate anyone who dares to cross his path.

The grim solution to this mayhem? To halt the Horseman's rampage, one must locate and obliterate his severed head.

The chilling sensation that ran through Graysen's veins left his blood running cold. The overall contents of this church's basement rendered him shocked. Bewildered, he simply couldn't grasp the magnitude of what was said! His mind raced through possibilities and considered whether this was a sick joke, a twisted prank? His Sleepy Hollow legend project proved so befuddling, confounding, and emotionally draining. Exasperated, he threw his hands up and bemused; what is the legend's truth?

While he tried to emotionally collect himself and regain his composure, his eyes caught the date inscribed on one of the papers. Looking up to the heavens in a state of sufferance, Graysen begged, "Please, dear God, save me!" as the date reads: "on the fateful evening of October 31, 2023." Today, today, today!!!

As he lamented and sobbed, "Today, today, today," he heard a loud thud upstairs. Dropping the paper, he ran to the door. Upon opening it, he witnessed a grimly deathlike sight. A figure on a black steed loomed before the entrance of the church. No head! Yes, no head on the rider's shoulders, but he clutched something in his hand.

Sheer terror raced through his veins, and dread consumed him. The Headless Horseman found him!?!

Filled with overwhelming fear, Graysen panicked. He slammed the door shut and locked it. He hoped the Horseman wouldn't catch sight of him or the door would hold him off. He searched the basement, looking for a way to escape undetected. He saw a minuscule window on the opposite wall, but it was too high and too tiny for him to fit through. The shadowy spot where the fireplace sat was cold and dark. On the right wall, the locked closet curiously bore no door handle. "Who has a door with no door handle? This place is too weird for the sane and rational!" he thought.

He was trapped! Yes, trapped! The only word that repeatedly raced through his mind was trapped!

The overwhelming sense of confinement made Graysen feel faint, but then he heard the Horseman's horse neigh and stomp outside. Bolting upright from a sudden surge of adrenaline running through his veins, Graysen intently listened to the Horseman's voice, muffled by the head he held in his hand.

"Where are you, Crane? Where is my head?"

Thoroughly dumbfounded and perplexed, Graysen realized that the revenge-driven Horseman mistook him for Ichabod Crane.  Stunned, Graysen, confounded and dazed, wondered how the Horseman could even be confused. He didn't bear any resemblance to Ichabod, at least not in his posted pictures. The more Graysen thought, the more he realized that the idea of the Headless Horseman confusing identities is ridiculous! He wore modern-style clothing, while Ichabod dressed in colonial garb. How absurd!

But then again, blindness or at least poor vision would account for the Headless Horseman's inability to distinguish between him and Ichabod. The Horseman, being headless, probably relied on his keen sense of smell and, yes, acute hearing to find his prey. In hindsight, Graysen grimly realized he had made a fatal mistake when he touched Ichabod's head.

He instantaneously recalled the moment he picked up one of the jars off the shelf. The ghastly sight of a severed head inside with its withered and decayed face was horrifying but still recognizable as Ichabod's, given the long nose, pointed chin, and terrified expression. Shocked and petrified, Graysen accidentally dropped the jar. It shattered when it hit the floor. Afterward, a dark, mysterious liquid from the jar splashed onto his trembling hand. Yuck!!! Revolting!!!

The preservative probably belongs to an evil realm where dark forces use black magic to brew liquids for malevolent and self-serving intentions. Oh!!! The witches brew most likely absorbed Ichabod's scent and transferred it onto him when it splattered. That's why the Horseman believed he was Ichabod.

Graysen cursed himself for being so careless. He wished he had never entered the church basement. Oh, what really awaited him later this evening? His enchantress scheduled the seance for this evening with a full Blood Moon hanging high in the sky at 3 a.m., the witching hour. He dressed as the Headless Horseman, and she, my Bride, sitting within a mysterious witch's circle in the Old Dutch Church cemetery. Oh, will he even survive any of this?

He regretted ever setting foot in this church and longed to reverse time. Roll it back and simply return to his New York City apartment after that first nightmarish dream. Oh, forget the nightmare. Go back to the encounter with the mischievous bookstore's prankster; that's when he should have seen it as a sign to turn around and move back to the city. Given the opportunity, he may even move back to his childhood home and never think of the Headless Horseman again! But now, he had to accept that it was too late to slip away and run back to any former residence. Yes, the harsh reality was that there was no turning back. He was trapped by the Headless Horseman, and he had to find a way to survive this nightmare.

The Headless Horseman stood squarely in front of the church door and fiercely pounded on it with his fist with an unyielding force. Seeing some wood crack and splinter under the Horseman's force reinforced the grave consequences Graysen now faced for trespassing.

Once again, the ghastly voice of the otherworldly phantom bellowed, "Give me back my head, Crane! Give me back my head!"

With only seconds left before the Horseman's imminent breach through the fortress, Graysen looked around desperately for something to defend himself with. He saw a candlestick on the table, but it was too light and flimsy to do any damage. The knife on the table was too dull and rusty to cut anything. The old book on the table was too fragile to effectively whack someone unconscious; woefully, it, too, was useless as a weapon. Getting ready to cry, Graysen found nothing useful, and despair started setting in.

Preparing to take his last stand, he grabbed the knife out of desperation and held it in front of him. He backed away from the door and slinked towards the fireplace. He hoped to ignite a fire to scare off or hurt the Horseman. If only he could find a way to somehow start it.

The door burst open with a

deafening bang! The Horseman stormed into the basement, gripping a pumpkin in one hand and brandishing a sword in the other. Barely fitting through the doorway, Graysen saw his horse squeeze through the narrow entrance. Absolutely spellbinding; the horse literally followed him inside.

The Horseman pointed his headless neck at Graysen. His demonic voice laughed and projected a sense of sheer apocalyptic pleasure as it filled the air.

"I found you, Crane! I found you!"

With a sense of determination enveloping him, the Horseman brandished his sword and lunged at Graysen.

Graysen screamed as he simultaneously threw his knife at him. As the knife flew through the air, it hit the Horseman in the chest. Pathetically, it merely ricocheted off him, yes, without even leaving a mark on his black coat. The Horseman's fiendish laughter filled the basement's air space as he continued his charge.

Graysen realized that his knife needed to be more effective against the Horseman. He needed something more powerful, something that could hurt or destroy him, a force of unparalleled strength. He remembered what he had read in the chilling papers on the table: the only way to stop him was to find his head and destroy it.

But how could he destroy it when he could not find his head? Oh, God!!! In desperation, he looked closer at the head the Horseman was holding in his hand only to find that the head he now carried belonged to Ichabod Crane.

Perplexed, overwhelmed, Graysen's head spun with a whirlwind of thoughts. In the interest of his own preservation, he asked himself how he could somehow use it to his advantage.

An idea sparked. Unleash the Horseman's fallibility. Make the Horseman make a mistake. Yes, a grave mistake that would have serious consequences.

Feeling like he had just got his

second wind, he charged toward the Horseman, skillfully dodging and evading the deadly slashes of his sword's swings. At one point, he vehemently grabbed the Horseman's arm to pull Ichabod's head away. Graysen hoped that his distractions would throw the Horseman off or create another opportunity for him to beat him back.

The Horseman resisted and relentlessly continued to swing and lunge his sword at Graysen. With a sudden burst of speed, he rushed forward to crush Graysen.

Holding on tight to Ichabod's head, Graysen summoned all of his force as he yanked harder. He felt Ichabod's head slip from the Horseman's grip. Snatching it, Graysen sprinted away from him.

He ran towards the fireplace, desperately searching for matches or a lighter. He planned to throw Ichabod's severed head into the fire. Hopefully, the head would burn, explode, or do something that would extensively harm the Horseman. Sadly, even worse luck awaited Graysen.

While some logs and ashes lay inside the fireplace, no matches or lighters were in sight!

He cursed under his breath. He had no way to light a fire. In looking back, he spotted the Horseman once again charging toward him.

As he charged, his black steed barreled toward him as well and then jumped over the table. In the ensuing chaos, he knocked over the candlestick and sent the papers scattering in the air.

Amidst this commotion, Graysen's eyes remained fixed on the Horseman's sword, its deadly swings catching the faint light.

In his desperate bid for a miraculous salvation and with every second slipping away, Graysen daringly threw Ichabod's head into the fireplace.

Thank God for small favors! A stroke of luck came his way, and he was blessed with a much-needed last-minute miracle. In a macabre twist, the severed head hit one of the logs only to recoil in a grotesque rock and roll dance. It rolled back and continued its grisly journey until it finally made contact with the candlestick.

What followed was beyond belief!

When the head made contact with the candlestick, an embedded device activated. It triggered a detonation signal, igniting a concealed pile of dynamite hidden under the table!

With an ear-piercing blast, the dynamite exploded! As the church and the basement rocked from the explosion, the floor collapsed. The ceiling caved. The windows shattered as the walls crumbled. Thick smoke from the fire filled the air.

Thrown back by the blast, Graysen slammed his head against the wall. Falling to the ground, a sharp pain surged through his chest, and his head spun. Desperately gasping for air as the suffocating and dense smoke quickly filled the basement's air space, he struggled to open his eyes. Squinting, he saw chaos and destruction lying before him. He could hear sirens going off in the distance.

As he tried to adapt to the spreading mayhem engulfing him, he noticed the Horseman near the fireplace. His lifeless figure, sprawled on the floor, lay motionless and covered with debris. His sword? Shattered in pieces. His black steed? Vanished!

With an overwhelming sense of joy and relief, Graysen realized that he had done it. He destroyed the Horseman. He stopped him.

Despite facing this fiery threat to his life, he felt emboldened to survive and euphoric about his accomplishments.

As he worked to shield himself from smoke inhalation, he cowered and tried to reposition himself by crawling. He felt terribly weak and became dizzy when he tried to sit up.

Floating in and out of consciousness, he positioned himself in a self-protect mode of covering his face with his shirt. After curling up into a ball, he worked to stop inhaling this toxic air by burying his head deep within his fetal position.

Undoubtedly, the rescue squad should arrive soon. He could hear fire sirens, trucks, and people screaming in the offing. His Katherine, his personal enchantress, should be here soon, too. He mused about what witches' incantations she used to save people trapped in these hellish predicaments.

While somewhat rolling around to ensure the correctness of his fetal position and other aspects of his hastily pulled-together self-protective stance, he felt something odd, hot, and creepy kind of abutting his back. Thinking it foolish to ignore the source, Graysen pulled out of his self-protective fetal position to see what it was. Squinting, he looked straight into the eyes of Ichabod Crane. Yes, it was his gruesome head that abutted his back!!!

Oh, God! Ichabod's head survived and was staring at him! Can you imagine a severed head ogling you? Now, totally sickened and perplexed, he wondered what he should do with it. Maybe he should donate it to the town? Keep it as a trophy, throw it away, or bury it somewhere?

Given the mayhem, he decided it was best for him to take a personal interest in what happened next. As he retreated into the fetal position, he kept his nose and mouth covered with his shirt. Then he narrowed his eyes to scrutinize Ichabod's face. The decapitated head's expression underwent a transformation. Aghast, Graysen didn't think he could survive this freak show! But no, Graysen relaxed. He was no longer terrified, nor was Ichabod Crane's facial expression displaying terror. Ichabod actually looked calm, truly at peace. Ichabod even seemed to smile at him.

In times like this, where a person is trapped in their circumstance, what else could Graysen do but smile back?

A voice in his head said, "Thank

you, Graysen. Thank you for freeing me from the Horseman's curse. Thank you."

Graysen recognized the voice as Ichabod's. While he was surprised, he was not scared. He also felt calm and connected with Ichabod, as though they shared a bond of friendship and gratitude. The newly hired Sleepy Hollow Gazette newspaper reporter replied in his mind. "You're welcome, Ichabod. You're welcome."

With that, his cell phone started ringing, but ringing somewhere out of his reach in this basement. Graysen wasn't going to attempt to find it, crawl to it. He lacked the strength to move. He was too weak. As he slipped into an unconscious state, his last fleeting thoughts were filled with hope. His cell could be a lifeline! Its ring a beacon for the rescue squad to find and save him!

Can the moonlight guide him

in his darkest hour,

through the shadows of his doom?

No! Therefore,

some truths are best left to the night and

dark little whispers of the wind!

## --The Bone Chilling End--

Brom Bones Van Brunt

Milton Keynes UK
Ingram Content Group UK Ltd.
UKHW050442230324
439902UK00015B/489

9 798224 207268